MEN WITHERING

Men Withering

FRANCIS MacMANUS

THE MERCIER PRESS
4, BRIDGE ST., CORK

First published 1939
This Edition 1966

Printed in the Netherlands
by N.V. Drukkerij Bosch-Utrecht

To my brother Brian

Contents

'Men Withering,' being the third volume of a trilogy about eighteenth-century Ireland, of which *'Stand and Give Challenge'* and *'Candle for the Proud'* were the first and second, respectively; and pity the poor author!

PART ONE

The Year's Burden

Pity the fool for whom life's cold as doom:
Colder far he'll find the enclosing stone
Of one poor grave, too mean for elbow-room,
Where tearless kin will leave him lie alone.

(From the Irish.)

'... I, dark in light, expos'd
To daily fraud, contempt, abuse and wrong,
Within doors or without, still as a fool,
In power of others, never in my own.'

(MILTON'S *Samson Agonistes*.)

'I will die bravely, like a bridegroom. What?
I will be jovial: come, come; I am a king,
My masters, know you that.'

(King Lear)

CHAPTER I

A little clay

I

The tree between the sheltering walls of the yard, a sycamore in full foliage, the only tree that thrived in the salt air of that place, began to unloose the million whispers that the warm evening coaxed from it with a touch.

He sank down in the wooden elbow-chair with his half-open right hand holding the six shillings on his lap, and sighed, nodding gravely, when at last, the footsteps of the scholar receding along the road from the tavern had become lost in the murmuring of the summer dusk and the leisurely ebbing of the sea. His brown coat and waistcoat, the cast-off clothing of a fuller man, crumpled up about his ears and thinly bearded jaws, so that his bald pate was almost cowled. The black kerchief which he used as a cravat was unknotted, and one end of it, hanging over an arm of the chair, wavered in the breeze that the unglazed window breathed in upon the room. Still nodding, and crooking his fingers nervously one by one upon the coins, he waited for the echoes in his mind to hush themselves completely until, in the quietness, thoughts would fall to him as gently as the grey light that, he knew, must now be drifting like fine blown dust behind the retreating day.

The remote babble of the echoes continued. His own voice seemed yet to be speaking the lines of the Latin verse which the scholar, who tried at the same time to shake off the fatigue of a day's work at the hay, repeated doggedly and translated into rapid bursts of Irish. Seldom had he met a lad so hungry for learning, so careful of every crumb as if a famine were about to destroy the scholarship of the earth; and in the autumn the lad would sail for the college in Bordeaux to become a priest, and maybe some day at the altar he would remember an old man who kept him at his books till there was no more light on the page. If all his scholars of the past sixty years remembered him, he would be a rich man indeed, but not in this world! He squeezed the six shillings in his fist. Surely this was the last money and the scholar was the last scholar, and since no more could be done, he should be satisfied. Gradually, as he waited listening, the inner voices mumbled to a monotone, faded, and his hearing was clear and ready for the comforting of the sea-swayed, sleep-giving air. He did not move a limb lest the tensing of dry muscles and the bending of stiff joints should break repose and remind him of the grave that could not now for long forego its claim upon him.

Beneath the window of the room, below in the tavern-yard, the talk of men rambled in undertones of Irish and broken English about the fishing, the saving of the hay, the hungry July, when potatoes grow scarce, and the chances of rain on the morrow. Fishermen and labourers they were, drinking ale together, listening indulgently to a man who had spoken good-humouredly once about how the French had freed themselves of tyrannous rulers. The man's accent was strange, and despite the under-current of laughter, there was a bite in the words. When a fisherman remarked that the French were a pack of murderers, thus repeating a phrase caught from a sermon, and that they had murdered their king some years before and also their queen who was only a woman, the stranger laughed, saying, 'Well, someone had to die.' Immediately, he called for more ale all round and began to talk about America, finishing up loudly with, 'It'll be thirty thousand years before we'll be treated justly and according to our rights, if we go on discoursing in this fashion and swilling beer.' Slow laughter again and the voices crept to silence and the stranger alone spoke, but too faintly to be heard.

The man in the room was rocking his body slightly in its bundle of clothes as if some inward pulsing were beginning to master his outward composure. A weak, sour smile curled the corners of his sunken mouth. A tired wind from the sea foraged stealthily in the foliage of the sycamore in the yard, and when it had gone over the village of Bunmahon, upward towards the mountains, he sat still once more but his calm did not return. He muttered, 'Let them! Let them talk!' He paused, cocking his head to hear what the stranger was saying down below, and then he began the muttering again, not continuously but fitfully, as if someone were interrupting.

'Let them talk! I could tell them more than they'd listen to. Let them argue and pretend they're fine men and that their ancestors were free on their own lands. That's all they're good for. That's all they'll ever do.

'I suppose you think that God Almighty made you to be ruled over by the gentry and the landlords and... Faith then, Donnacha Mac Conmara could tell you that. He did not. Oh! but you wouldn't listen to me. I'm only an old man. I'm only an old fool babbling to himself in an empty room. But you don't know the things I've seen. There was famine and I lived through it. I saw people fighting for their bits of farms, but you wouldn't do that. The good men are all dead, and I'm left. They're all dead. Why am I left after them all? Why am I left? O God in Heaven, I'm going cracked, conversing here with myself and the dead. Why am I left?'

Tears rolled down his cheeks and he rocked backwards and forwards, beating time with the fist that held the shillings. Unknown to himself the flowing whispering of the sea soothed his distress, and his mind, free, began to busy with scraps and phrases of a lament that he had been trying to piece together. For a friend it was, who had died that year, in April, and some day a mason with clever hands would carve the words on fine stone which would be set above the grave, three, four miles away in Ballylaneen. Already he could see and read what the mason would cut: the name, the day, the month and the year, 1795; and beneath would begin, for all to read as long as stone lasted: *Thaddeus hic situs est.* He wondered, grinning, how Tadhg Gaolach O Suilleabhain would like his name in the Latin, Tadhg who hardly knew a word of it except stray bits from the Mass, *Dominus vobiscum* and the like, and it wrong. They had found him in Waterford in the big church, it was said, dead at his prayers, and it was as he had always desired: a holy death in a holy place; and they had carried his body all the way from the city; and so another poet was buried. *Thaddeus hic situs est:* Tadhg lies here. A little clay, a pinch, covers a great poet. *Illustrem vatem parvula terra tegit.* That was a good line, yet not good enough for Tadhg. *Plangite, Pierides.* Weep, muses, weep whoever it was that gave men song. Weep! – *Plangite:* the word resounded like stringed instruments all stroked together of a sudden as a beginning of deep, grief-laden music such as would be played for a great dead king, and the music, rising, wailed through the words. *Quis canet Erindum laudes, quis facta virorum?* Who will sing praise of Ireland, who the deeds of her men? Who will sing? They had all gone one by one, the poets, and he in truth must be among the last of them; so that there would be no one in the end, not even a scholar, to remember and write for a stone, a name and a date and a single lamenting line. *Plangite, Pierides.*

The words scattered and reformed in his mind like a flock of birds taken in a gust, but he could not bring them together to make them fly strong and sure with the sense he desired. They vanished in the mood that seemed to move in his blood, out from his heart. The sea-wind had stirred the tree again, and this time he followed the wind inland, up the countryside to where the packed mountains shouldered off the sky, until he was with his son and his grand-children, in their cabin on the treeless slope. He nodded briskly, as if to welcome. If, he thought, a man had one foot in the grave, the best thing for him would be to go and sit down among his own people, because it was a lie to say that men, as they grew older, feared death and loneliness less; and strangers did not care much how comfortably you died so long as you died quickly. But he would have a good funeral, without expense to anyone.

He thrust his hand inside his shirt to find the leather purse, strung on a cord around his neck. He opened the purse, fingered the five sovereigns and odd shillings it contained and counted into it the scholar's money. As he did so, his elbow struck his stick which rattled on the bare boards of the floor. Hastily, he slipped the purse inside his shirt again, buttoned his waist-coat, and with a low groan stooped to fumble for the stick and the high-crowned hat that lay underneath the chair.

The fishermen and the labourers were leaving the yard, and the stranger, with a laugh deep in his throat, was saying that he would meet them again another night. The man in the room was listening. 'Hey, Tomás,' he heard, 'bring me another. I'll sit here awhile. It's too warm yet for sleep.'

He guided himself along by the wall, feeling plaster crumbling, and took the creaking staircase cautiously step by step down to the yard, to the wooden seat beneath the window. He was breathing heavily as he let himself down to the seat. He lay back against the dusty, dry ivy-tendrils that clung to the wall. The stranger was beside him.

II

'I beg your pardon,' said the stranger, in English, and moved over to make room on the seat. For a second he remained at ease, and then, rustling against the ivy, he scraped his feet nervously in the dust. 'They keep good ale here,' he said. 'Will you drink with me, sir?'

'I thank you, sir. I thank you kindly. But ale and myself...'

'Wine, then. Let it be red wine of some kind.'

'Now, if you don't mind...'

'Brandy? Brandy it is. Tomás! Tomás.' The tavern-keeper,

soft-footed, stood in the doorway. 'A glass of brandy for this gentleman.'

'Gentleman?'

'Brandy. Put it down to me. Ah! this is the perfect place for resting.'

'You'd be a stranger to this side of the country, I'd say.'

'Yes and no! I'm travelling with some German spectacles that I'd like to part company with; but at a price, you know. At a price! But since the folk in these parts will not bid farewell with their money, I fear I must keep to my bad companions. Would you like to try a pair?'

'No! No, sir! Thank you kindly.'

'Here is the brandy for the gentleman,' said the tavern-keeper.

'They haven't any money, sir,' the old man added, sharply.

He gripped the glass that the tavern-keeper placed against his hand and after clinking the rim against the stranger's beer-mug, he eagerly raised the liquor, sniffed and sipped. Tomás stood by and said, 'Would you like a bite before bed, Mr. Hume?'

In Irish the old man broke in: 'Leave a sup of milk and a bit of bread upstairs for me, will you, Tomás? I'll pay you all right. My scholar went to-night. That's a good man, Tomás.'

'Oh! I suppose I will. But mind you, next week...'

'I'll be gone, Tomás. I'm going home if I can get a cart or a lift northward at all.'

'Home,' Tomás sniggered, turning away into the house.

Mr. Hume drank and clapped his empty mug down on the seat. He stared at the inert figure beside him and noted how ghostly pale in the glimmer of the night was the countenance with its fringe of scant beard. A door inside the house was banged, Tomás ground out a few oaths harshly, and a dog scampered out across the yard.

'Do you make your rounds, Mr. Hume,' the old man asked, 'by coach or by horseback?'

'I prefer to walk it like Adam; sometimes the stage-coach, outside of course, when I can afford it.'

'It's well to be young and travelling. Aye, indeed. I travelled a fair share of the world myself, on foot. I know every inch of this part of Munster. They know me too, but I don't know them; the people, I mean, sir. I've lived too long. More than sixty years ago I was a young man like yourself — here's to your health! — and I walked these roads and roads on the Continent, and I was in Newfoundland, too: the Land of the Fish, that is, sir, as we call it. You're a young man, now, aren't you?'

'Not young enough for a designing young widow, nor too old for breaking my heart on the glance of an ingenuous coquette.'

'They're fine words. Ah! but you're only a child.'

'You've seen many changes, I'm sure.'

'I have then, sir, but not so many that I wouldn't recognise the world that's in it now. It's true that once, long ago, the people daren't let on they were going to Mass of a Sunday, and schoolmasters like myself were no favourites of the law-men. I beg your pardon, sir, but maybe I'm offending...'

'Not at all. I'm a Presbyterian. I'm convinced that it's a crime...'

'A crime it is, sir. Here we are, sir, paying tithes to Protestant clergymen, and paying rents for holes and corners of farms, and three-quarters of us never thinking if there's a right or wrong in the matter at all. And look it, sir, there's a man up in Carrick, one of the gentry, and he's feared worse than the blackest devil out of hell. Do you know what he did one market-day? Do you know what he did? He tied two men with ropes to a cart and flogged the backs off them. Himself did, with his own hands and whip. He did.'

'You've spilled your brandy. May I call for another.'

'No, no, thank you. No, sir, thank you.' In confusion the old man muttered, sitting up stooped. The fire in him had been fire that could find little nourishment in so dry a body, and quickly he became composed and, still breathless, he began to speak again:

'For many a year of my life, sir, I hoped to die glad. What man doesn't have the hope? I hoped to see the world changing for the better and the people stirring themselves again. Maybe I don't understand things, but I'm sure the people are too far gone now. They're withered. There's little left of the old stock. Up in Dublin there's a parliament and we hear of gentlemen making speeches, but what good are speeches to poor people, poor dogs that only want to fill their bellies? Let sleeping dogs lie. They're used to the whip and the kicking boot. They won't even bark. And, mind you, sir, there was a time when they did lift a hand. I saw men fighting with sticks and stones for a few acres of grazing, but they were beaten and they lay down, and now... ah! let the dogs lie and sleep and eat and tumble into the grave where there are no rents to be paid. All I want myself is to sit and not mind anyone.'

Casually, Hume replied, 'The French didn't lie down, I believe.'

'I heard that kind of talk. They murdered their king. They're cursed from the altars.'

'We haven't any king to murder; at least, George is not one of our own.'

'The French kept together.'

Then briskly, rising to his feet suddenly, Hume said, 'We can unite. We can, sir. We can unite.'

'We? But you're a gentleman, sir!' As he spoke, the old man heard a stir in the doorway, and instantly he murmured to Hume, 'Trade in German spectacles is bad, as you say. They have no money. And besides they have good eyesight, like Tomás there at the door.'

'Oh!' Hume answered. 'Is that you, Tomás?'

'Don't be interrupting, Donnacha Mac Conmara,' Tomás rapped out in Irish. 'The gentleman was talking.'

In English Donnacha said, 'I'll be going to bed now, Mr. Hume. I'm getting chilled. These old bones of mine have the winter in them for marrow. It must be near midnight anyway.'

Hume stepped up to him and placed a hand on his shoulder. 'May I help you upstairs, sir. A light, Tomás, a candle.'

Donnacha shook off the hand gently. 'I'm all right, Mr. Hume. I don't need a candle. Thank you all the same. God bless your heart.'

With his left hand on the wall, he went into the house and climbed the stairway, pausing on every step to make sure of a footing on the next, and sniffing at the close air that held dead the odours of beer, damp flooring, lately baked bread and salted fish. His shuffling feet and tapping stick raised up a succession of hollow and inhospitable echoes. When he reached the room he fingered the darkness and felt with his knees the edge of the low bed. Cautiously he swept his hand across a box that served as table till he found a piece of dry bread and a cup. He began to mumble the bread with the few stumps of teeth that remained in his gums. Dry fragments trickled down his beard and coat. His ears were open to the voices from the yard.

Hume was talking, his voice full of his rapid eager energy, but only the loud gob-wide replies of Tomás mounted distinctly to the room.

'Aye! a schoolmaster, begod, without a school,' Tomás was saying. 'They say he was a poet once, but I wouldn't put much pass on what people say. Would you, sir? He just wanders around, picking up a penny here and there. He'll be getting out of this as soon as he can cadge a lift on a cart. Did you hear him about going home? He can't live much longer anyway. – No, sir. A bit cranky.' Then a guttural laugh. 'God bless your eyes, sir. A candle, is it? Why Mr. Hume, he's stone blind.'

He pulled up the clothes around him, and lying as straight as his stiff joints would allow him, he stroked his forehead with a thin hand.

Tomás crossed the yard, wheeled a cart over the cobbles, closed the creaking yard-gate, stood whistling softly for a minute and then, returning to the house, locked the door below with a clinking of chains. In another room, boards groaned under quietly moving feet. Presently the house was full of the sea-surge and the hiss of the unresting sycamore leaves.

They say he was a poet once. Picking up a penny here and there.

Instinctively he burrowed his head down among the clothes to shut out the refrain. It was queer how loss of the eyes made the ears keener and thronged the mind with echoes, tired and confused like the gab of a rabble at the end of its tether in a tavern. Damn Tomás! He would sleep. O, but he would sleep and forget. His breathing troubled him then and he coughed out in little gasps and heard, resignedly, the wheezing of the air in the confines of old lungs. He turned over on his side and shifted the hard purse on the string from beneath his ribs.

Mouths gabbled at him out of the dark.

Picking up a penny here and there. Illustrem vatem parvula terra tegit. They say he was a scholar once. A blind man can't read in the books. Blind or old, I'm a better man than the best. Good morrow, Mr. Hume. Brandy for the gentleman. Plangite, Pierides. Don't forget me lad when you're ordained. Who will sing? Young I was and she was fair, and through the woods we went. Plangite, plangite, plangite, plangite,...

Submissive to it all, he lay still, and all of it, even the bell-like word clanging for tears, faded. *Parvula terra,* he whispered, and coughed shortly. The little pinch of clay! The dry rustle of his own whisper delayed on his hearing. He shivered.

The dread of mortality, the terror of the inevitable shrouding of the body, fanned him icily, till shrinking like a cat from the cold outer-world to the warmth before the fire, he wished desperately in his half-sleep for everlasting shelter against the inappeasable winds of death. He could feel them, those ceaseless winds, flowing about him, crumbling him as a desiccate lump of earth is crumbled in a heavy rainfall, pulverising him back into the dust from which he had come; and so they had been flowing, year after year, minute by minute, while the flesh bloomed healthily and then shrank to a wrinkled casing and the hair fell from the shining pate, and the bones became almost as jointless as boughs; and he, with every desire withered except the desire to live, groped and reached forward along his earthly course with an apprehensive stick. As he sank now into his half-animal sleep, his fingers twitching on the blanket, he carried with him the thought of his own decay as though it were the destiny of the people among whom he lived. He was going. So were they.

They ate, drank, slept, grew sick, bore children, quarrelled, made peace, died, and were satisfied. On the harsh weather-scarred slopes of mountains and along boggy acres, in houses and cabins built of mud against supporting ditches, in hovels that were too warm and suffocating now with the accumulated heat of the day as they would be biting cold in the brawling wintry weather, in these shelters there were men stripped of youth and old before their time, women who in hunger had borne children, and children who had begun to accept as immutable the hardship of their lives; and now they turned in sleep on the straw, or lay deadly still, or suffered wordlessly the weeping of the very young and the hungry, or listened to the cries of their beasts, stabled with them on the house floors, and to the innumerable busy life in the furze thatch; or watched the faint far stars through gaps in the roof and wondered, for a moment, whether there ever had been anything else for them and their kind other than straw, mud walls, potatoes, and sleep with the beasts of the field.

Donnacha turned on his back and lay with his mouth open. Dreams mingled. He saw what he had seen so often before he went blind: stonewalled, slated houses and mansions, some decayed with broken windows and pocked blistered woodwork, standing aloof at the ends of grassgrown avenues and drives; some kept neat, the walks gravelled and the windows curtained; and he saw himself walking the drives, going warily in dread of dogs, slipping around to an outhouse or to the kitchen-door to stand with his hat twirling in his fingers, and saying, to a servant or a lackey, 'Please, sir,' and 'I beg of you, sir,' and 'Would your honour please give a poor man a bit of bread or a scrap of meat?' Even in his sleep his hands moved to touch his forehead in obsequious salute.

He awoke, struggling to sit up.

The yard-gate was banged resoundingly. Horses clip-clapped across the cobbles and a voice, sharp and irate, went through the house. Tomás was answering gruffly from below, growling that he was coming with a light. From the patter of footsteps, the iron shuffling of the horses and the muddle of voices, the old man picked out the jingle of spurs.

Rubbing his forehead foolishly with the palm of his hand, he settled back on the bed, and then he felt the change in the air. As sleep crept over him again, he heard dimly a door banging, footsteps pounding heavily on the stairs, then Hume's lively voice, and finally, Tomás saying: 'Some soldiers, sir. Drunk as maggots. The rest will be here to-morrow.'

Small clouds were driving in from the sea, carrying a fine and refreshing rain.

I V

In the morning he sat on a shaft of the cart in the yard, feeling the freshness of the washed air on his face and knowing the brightness of the sun as a nebulous pale curtain only, shifting and shadowing before his dead eyes. Of the murk of the night's dreaming, there was not even a wisp in his memory. The disquieting desire to go northwards, to the mountains, to his people, remained.

He was immobile, his head bent on his hands and his hands supporting themselves on his stick, until this desire, and a sourness in his stomach turned by the old milk on which he had broken fast, gave him acute discomfort. He arose to walk, and sighed against a cramp in his meagrely fleshed thighs.

Back and forth, tapping walls and gables with his stick, he trapesed from the cart to the road gateway where, on every occasion, he stood to listen. On one of these journeys, he heard the rumbling of cart-wheels, muffled in the dust. He took his stand in the middle of the road and prodded around him ostentatiously with his stick.

'Heigh! Will you get out of the way out of that?' said the carter in Irish.

'Give me a hand, if you please, sir. I don't know what direction to take.'

'Walk to your left. That's it. To your left. There's the wall.'

'Would you be going north, sir? The way it is with me, I'm too stiff to do much walking. But many a time I...'

'I'm not going north. There now, keep against the wall.'

'Would you be going north at all, sir? Wait a minute and tell me.'

'Keep back or you'll be dog's meat. I tell you I'm not going north.'

Donnacha cringed back against the wall, his back pressed against the stones, while the cart rolled past. 'You ill-mannered pup,' he said, raising his voice as the cart went farther away. 'But what do you know? When your kind were bondmen, my kin were your masters.' Instantly, he checked himself, grinned at his own poor show of temper, and returned to the yard and his seat on the cart-shaft.

'My kin were your masters,' he muttered, wondering whether his kind had ever been any better as lords than the gentry of foreign blood in the big houses. Touched by the thought as violin-strings are touched by wayward fingers, his memory released confusedly an old, half-forgotten piece of verse about the high days of the lords of Ireland, their houses and their hospitality to men of learning, clerics and poets. The verse sang up in broken lines and so he came to serenity. He was sitting thus, twining and untwining his long narrow fingers on the head of his blackthorn stick, when a voice disturbed him with 'I beg your pardon.'

It was Hume. 'I beg your pardon,' he repeated. 'Please do not stand up. Oh! please do not stand up for me. I want to apologise for any unkind word I uttered last night. It was an accident, I assure you. When I offered to find you a candle, I was not aware...'

'That's all right, Mr. Hume. I knew you were a gentleman,' Donnacha replied, almost hurt by the kindness in Hume's voice. He laughed. 'But you're a very fine gentleman to be selling spectacles!'

Hume chuckled. 'Very fine gentlemen often have sold worse wares.'

'Themselves, by heavens.' They laughed together. 'You'll not do much in the way of business in these parts,' Donnacha added. 'I mean in spectacles, sir.'

'I can try,' said Hume. 'There are some houses in the neighbourhood, and a clergyman or two.'

'Don't be talking about the French to the likes of them. If myself were listening to you long enough, you might convert me. But not them. Not in a thousand years.'

Hume was grave. 'No,' said he. 'Talking about the French is a very dangerous pastime for an honest trader.' He began to take rapid steps to and fro, always turning sharply on the ball of his foot, crunching the gravelled dust as he did so. In an undertone, he continued, 'They aren't so much afraid of the French as the example of the French.'

'They?'

'Oh! you know as well as I do. The gentry, the lords, the squires, call them what you will. They possess both the wealth and the power to make this nation prosperous and free but they use neither to that end. They fritter away their time here in the country with hunting and wenching, endless swilling of claret and rum-punch, and quarrelling like dogs about the bare bone they call honour. They had their opportunity when they were volunteers mustered in defence of their country. What did they win? Legalities, sir. What satisfies them? The gout, sir, and the pox, and half-a-dozen rapier scars from most honourable duels.' Hume snapped his fingers. 'But they know in their hearts that some day, as happened in France, they will be obliged to slaughter or be slaughtered by a people armed...' Hume leaned against the cart and drummed his fingers on the spoke of a wheel.

'I don't understand all the English you spoke, Mr. Hume. But pardon me, it sounds dangerous. What good will it do, anyway? What good did blood-spilling ever do? The country is at peace. I saw the bad days. I carry them on my back like a bag.'

'Surely,' said Hume between his teeth, 'you do not wish to have the bag, the devil's bag, passed on as a legacy!'

'As long,' Donnacha replied rapidly, saying whatever came into his mind, 'as long as we have a bite and cover for the night, we're safe; we're fortunate; we're prosperous. What would the priest say to that kind of talk? Didn't the French murder and burn and... Mr. Hume, speak low. Tomás, I think...'

'Yes,' Hume murmured. 'He was in the doorway. He's gone now.'

'Don't trust him, sir. Those speeches of yours could be exchanged for King's money. And the soldiers are here!'

'So I've been told,' Hume said. 'They'll not be here to-morrow, I believe.' Then, suddenly, he leaned down to the old man and whispered, 'Will you do me a favour? You see, when I make my rounds I like to have every pocket lined well with my goods. Then, with a flourish which is part of the trade I can pull out spectacles for every manner of complaint. Now, I happen to have a packet of private letters which I hold very dear. They're quite private, I swear to you. They take up much room in my pocket. I should be obliged to you if you would take charge of them till I return to-night or perhaps, in the morning. I'd rather not leave them in my room. Tomás pries too much. Besides, these soldiers are no respecters of the property they are paid to protect. Do I ask too...?'

'You're asking nothing, sir. Nothing at all. They're safe with me. I can't read them anyway.'

Hume pressed closer to Donnacha and thrust a bulky packet into the left-hand pocket of his coat. Then, into one of the palms resting on the knob of a blackthorn stick he pressed a coin. The thin fingers closed greedily. 'A sovereign, sir?' said Donnacha. 'A whole sovereign?' He coughed for breath with excitement. 'I can go miles. I can go miles now.'

'Drink my health to-day and to-morrow,' Hume said quietly. 'And may I ask for one more favour. If you do not mind, please say a prayer for me.' Then, Hume, with quick decisive steps was gone.

A hush, like the silence left after an army has marched by in haste, possessed the yard.

Involuntarily, Donnacha Ruadh pulled himself to his feet and turned his head from side to side. A vague alarm of oncoming menace moved him. All he remembered of the man who had walked away down the road, was an orderly strong assault of words and he tried to fix his mind on them. There was new hope in them, he surmised, as heartening and yet as frightening as a wandering light far-out in a bog is to a lost man. But what was it? What in the name of God was the sense of it? He relaxed to his seat on the shaft. The old broken verse about the lords of Ireland in their hey-day, welled up and drowned all questioning with slow regret and black lamentation for the dead.

V

The yard, in the afternoon, was crammed with the soldiers. They jostled about, sullen and ill-tempered after their march in the sun, and having listened to their superiors, dispersed to the houses and cabins on which they were billeted.

Later, they returned. Grumbling about their quarters they were then; cursing, ripe for brawling. The old man did not know where to take cover, for they made their own of every room in the house. He tried to escape from the yard, from the dust and the hoarse, disgruntled babble. Hands contemptuously pushed him hither and thither, and voices, some English, some Irish – for the men were regulars – called him grandfather. When he staggered among them, tapping and searching for some firm place in all the world, a whine coming into his breathing, he could smell spirits and beer. He recognised their mood. They wanted a figure for their fun, a figure that would protest sufficiently but not excessively against their baiting. A woman would suit. But he would have to do, and he blind and cowering.

'I say,' one cried, 'you're very friendly-like in these parts.'

'Aren't we afraid, boys?' shouted another. 'He's a Frenchie.'

'Aye, by God. A Marsalaisy man.'

'No, he's a United man. Can't you see his disguise? A United Irishman. Give him the pegging-top.'

Then he was caught, wrenched into a spin, and pushed. Toppling with weakly waving arms he called hoarsely for help, crying that they would kill him. He found himself held up, shaken like a sack, and suddenly let go to the ground. He sprawled on his face on the gravel, breathing dust into his nostrils and licking it to slime on his spittled lips. He whispered desperately a succession of pleas to the Mother of God, and on the heels of those pleas hot angry blasphemies came running as the outcry of his soul in its utter helplessness. The yard was full of laughter and shouting and the scurrying of booted feet. He heard Tomás – and Tomás, too, was laughing. That startled him into movement. His right fist scraped in rubble for the knob of the stick which he found, gripped and held. He raised himself on all-fours. A foot pressed him down again. He sat. They pulled him prostrate on his back. He lay, talking incoherently, one half of his heart wanting to tell them they were no men, no soldiers, but scum, spineless drunken cowardly scum; and the other half, too strong for him, made him plead and rave that they'd murder him, a poor sightless man, who had never harmed a soul and who was loyal from head to foot to His Majesty, George of England. They left him there to blow muddied dust from his lips and when they had trooped into the tavern, he dragged himself on hands and knees till he reached a wall and could stand upright once more. His begrimed fists beat on the wall against which he cooled his face, and he wept like a child in whom some dream has been broken and the heart blackened: 'O Jesus, have mercy and bring me home!'

Afterwards, he was stretched on the half-dunged straw in the corner of the yard, stupefied, hearing only the indifferently endless sighing of the tree overhead, when a man approached. He covered his face with his arms and moaned, 'Ah! Ah!'

'Don't be afraid, Mac Conmara. It's only your friend Tomás. Come on now and I'll give you a good bite to eat. Come on now, like a good man. The lieutenant himself wants a word with you. Up dining and wining with the magistrate he was and he's in a grand humour. And look,' said Tomás, still speaking Irish, but now sharply, 'you'll have to find a bed somewhere else to-night. Your room's taken. Come on now. That's the man.'

Roughly he hauled Donnacha to his feet and holding his shoulders, guided him across the yard.

'Don't let them hurt me. Ah! Tomás, don't let them.'

'They won't hurt you, man. Most of the soldiers are gone, too,' Tomás said confidently. 'They went on some business or other. All you have to do is to give straight honest answers to whatever the officer will ask you. You're an honest man, we all know. Aren't you now? He's sitting in the parlour with the magistrate. There now, lift your foot at the step.'

'What do I know, Tomás? What could I tell fine gentlemen?'

He was led into the room and by sounds and stirrings he sensed the presence of the four men in it, the officer, the magistrate and two guards.

'This is him, your honour,' said Tomás in English from the doorway. The door was closed.

'Stand there.' The voice was young, deep, slow with wine, yet commanding. 'Move that candle closer, Mr. Felton. Damn this handwriting.' Paper rustled and the table was slapped. 'Now, Mr. Felton, as magistrate of this place, you must be acquainted with the people. Proceed.'

'Thank you, lieutenant.' Mr. Felton spoke softly, paused, sniffed at a pinch of snuff feverishly, snapped the lid of the box shut and hemmed with satisfaction. Donnacha Mac Conmara detected a weariness in the tones, a mild disgust with life, and as he listened, trying to pierce into the man who spoke the stealthily soft words, his nerves steadied. 'The lieutenant,' continued Mr. Felton, 'gave me some information to-day... by the way, you understand English. Good! Excellent!' Hands were rubbed together, palm flat against palm. 'We shall get along famously, you and I. Well, as I was saying, the lieutenant gave me some information which only bears out my own fears. And now, I believe that you are decent and, shall we say highly respected? You can help us by...'

'Mr. Felton,' broke in the lieutenant harshly, 'wants to question you. Answer directly, sir. You are a perfectly, loyal subject of His Majesty, are you not? There are traitors abroad these days. Have you met with or heard of any man who spreads sedition? Have you heard anyone speaking in favour of the damned French? Have you, sir? Cease the trembling. Speak up.'

'It's only foolish talk and chatter, your honour.'

'Then' – and the table jerked from its place as the lieutenant leaned forward – 'then you have heard such talk. By God you have.'

'I mean, your honour, that...'

'Don't lie in my teeth, you old ruffian. Answer me directly.'

'Pardon me, lieutenant,' Mr. Felton interrupted, his silken tone unchanged. Donnacha Ruadh instinctively turned to him for protection. 'If I may say so, this man...'

'These people are born liars, Felton. No! they know nothing. Absolutely nothing! They've heard nothing. They've seen nothing. They're blind, deaf and dumb. And there's hardly a young man in the place. Out fishing, the women say. Egad, sir, it's convenient – Well, you, answer at once.'

The magistrate tapped his snuff-box and snuffed quickly.

'I'm blind, your honour. I never heard anything. The only stranger I know is Mr. Hume. Yes, that's his name, I think.'

The lieutenant relaxed in his chair and grunted. Wine, decanted from a height, bubbled into a glass, and splashed on the floorboards. Felton murmured, 'No, thank you,' and the lieutenant drank hastily, sucked his breath with a chirp through his teeth and grunted. 'This Hume?'

Felton continued to murmur. 'An honest, loyal trader with a merry disposition. His levity would prevent him from sinking into sedition of any kind. His letters of introduction were excellent in nature and origin. Why, he attended the Lord Lieutenant himself in Dublin.' Then, raising his voice, he added, 'Please do not be frightened. Put down your hands, Mr. Mac Namara. Isn't that your name? Lieutenant Greaves wishes to fulfil his duty, that is all. Now, have you heard of any group or body of men or society at work in this district or outside it? You do hear some gossip, I'm sure.'

'Your honour, on my oath, I swear before God...'

'That's sufficient, Mr. Mac Namara... Have you ever heard of the United men, the United Irishmen, Mr. Mac Namara? Oh! I'm afraid not.'

'Cease this, Mr. Felton. This man is not a child,' said Greaves, pushing back his chair and striding across the room. Donnacha retreated, shuffling. 'If you are concealing any information, you'll pay for it. Speak up. Tell what you know this instant. Keep your confounded hands down from your face, you reprobate. What are you concealing? You know something. Will you stop moving?'

'Oh! your honour, your honour, your honour...'

The door was opened, a soldier entered and clicked heels. 'Reporting, sir. We found one, down on the sands, hiding. We have him under guard outside. Sergeant O'Brien found arms in a cottage.'

'That's good. That's excellent.'

'A musket and some pike-heads, sir.'

Greaves laughed deeply. 'Take this old fool out,' said he, 'and leave him in the tap-room. Tap-room? A piggery! Bring in the other, the prisoner.' The wine bubbled again into the glass. 'This, as you may perceive, Mr. Felton, is not easy work.'

There were five or six men in the tap-room and they were drowsy and subdued with beer. One of them called out, 'Here comes grandfather again. Sit by me, grandfather. There's no ill-will.' Donnacha was placed sitting with his back to the wall.

A mug was pressed into his hand and he held the handle shakily, dropping the liquor upon his breeches. He lifted his mug when they told him, and drank obediently, dribbling upon his beard with the fright that still was on him, and then, not tasting the beer at all, he sat inertly, to contemplate his own enveloping darkness with his deserted eyes. At the end of a few minutes, having forgotten his presence, the soldiers conversed in short half-finished sentences about their billets and their pay, their boots and women, about France and the rumours of her victorious armies, and about the miseries of marching, and of all they said he gave no sign of having heard one word. By and by one of them noticed that the mug was swinging by the handle between his fingers and that the beer was spilling and hissing across the dry boards of the floor, and this soldier said, 'Hey, old man, you're losing your beer.' A comrade rapped out, 'Leave him alone. Can't you see he's crying about something.' Even then Donnacha Ruadh did not hear. So they let him be.

And why his heart was sickened with hollow, dusty weeping he could not have told no more than a child that, beaten for mischief long past and long forgotten, can explain why grief should be thrown upon it of a sudden.

'Come, old fellow,' said a soldier. 'There's fun in the yard. You'll see something.'

He followed them to the yard door. The beer, swallowed down to an empty stomach, had made him a little giddy.

The place around the tree in the yard was packed with men. Only a few of them spoke. One called for the lantern to be brought closer and another asked for a rope to be knotted twice. The lieutenant was talking, rapidly, over beside the tree and his words flowed like a torrent that rattles and grinds pebbles in its sweep. Then he ceased, and the yard was menacingly still.

Donnacha Ruadh felt the terror. He groped and held a shoulder. 'What are you doing with me, an old man like me?'

'Be quiet. It's not you, old fellow. We've younger game.'

'What's happening at all?'

'Shut your mouth.'

'Fire away,' said the lieutenant in the yard. On the instant, expecting danger to himself at the sound of that voice, Donnacha tensed his body.

A faint forlorn hiss, a dull crack like the flip of a wet rag, and then another crack almost upon it. A cry, high-pitched, breaking. A cold whistle of breath.

'Jesus!' said a soldier.

'He'll not give in.'

'I'll give you four to one he will.'

The hiss; the indefinite slap; the breath streaming out under shock: all again.

Beer as bitter as sloes retched back into Donnacha's throat. Blood was swirling in his head. 'They have,' explained the man at his elbow, 'a young lad tied to the tree. A United Marsalaisy as sure as a gun.'

'Where's Mr. Felton?'

'Who?'

'The magistrate.'

'He's not here. Hold your tongue or you'll get a back-lashing too.'

The soft, plobby cracking again and the protesting grunted breath. Donnacha Ruadh stopped counting.

'Now,' Greaves said, 'will you speak?... Go on, give him more. Give it to him.'

The soldiers in the doorway pressed forward.

'He's a pig for blood,' said one.

'There's plenty flowing now.'

Donnacha, through a dull hub-bub in his ears, heard the lash at work again, sighing in the air with intense delight and slapping wet flesh and he heard, too, Greaves calling out ruffian and scoundrel and screaming that the prisoner would get a leather tongue. In his heart he was saying that there was nobody in the yard, that the yard did not exist, and that he was only making up, out of past days of survived anguish, a nightmare that would vanish as soon as he shook his head and shouted back the real world again, where the wind blew and the sea spread over the world and fires burned small and snug on mountain hearths.

However it was that the man at the tree strained in his ropes, the soldiers broke into an excited murmur. Then in Irish, the man at the tree spoke: 'Stop! Let me free.' Because he was not understood, or perhaps because he was only half heard, he was

28

not heeded. But Donnacha Ruadh heard and understood, and his mind, filled with insane imaginings of what was being done to the prisoner and deprived of the restraining sight of his eyes saw flesh bared to the bone and sopping with blood. His forehead was wet and cold with the sweat of sickness. A thick, warm liquid clotted and burned in his throat. It was then, despite himself, that he screamed hoarsely.

A hand was clapped over his mouth, his arms were gripped close to his ribs and he was dragged back into the house, out to the hallway and thrust hard against the wall while the door was being opened. It was done quickly.

The door was opened, he was pushed, kicked behind and sent sprawling into the dust of the road. Face downward, he flopped about with his hands, searching from habit for his lost stick. He raised himself to his knees, then to his feet, and with his hands before him in the darkness, went past the house, swerving and staggering from the stone walls and twigs of the hedge. His hat was gone. He halted for a moment to feel his bald pate with his hands, beat his hands together and groaned, and stepping onward again, he blundered against a wall, slithered down to the grass and lay with his face in his arms. All his being cried out for the dark and for unbroken repose. Cries from the tavern set him moving once more. By gripping the stones of the wall, he pulled himself to his feet, and crouching, his hearing guiding him down the road to the wash of the sea, he began a pitiable, half-toppling trot. Fear urged him. Death, he felt, was padding along behind in the dust, swaying when he swayed, stopping when he stopped, and waiting patiently for the final blow. He lifted his voice and called for protection on his son whom he had not seen for so many years, on his son's children and on dead friends whose passing he had in his terror forgotten, and he called on his daughter to guide him because he was lost and wandering. In hopelessness he cursed them, as if they, far away, had heard and failed him.

Still crying, he was stumbling in a few minutes, across sand-dunes, tottering out to the incoming wavering fringes of foam.

CHAPTER II

The fox

I

A fisherman, lying in a stone, mud-plastered cabin in the lee of outcropping rocks, heard the old crazy crying from the beach and wondered sleepily what dead thing it was that the birds fought and clawed over in the darkness. But his wife had heard, too, and she shook him, telling him to rise and run down to the sand or someone would be lost in the sea.

'No! it wasn't the birds,' she said, white-faced. 'He called once or twice, God help him, whoever he is.'

The fisherman pulled on his breeches and ran bare-foot down to the sand. The light was thin and grey. He peered and saw the old man lying, face upward, in a pool of water. Quickly he hoisted the sodden bundle to his shoulders and surprised at its lightness, returned to the cabin where his wife, with a rush-light lit, looked out intently into the night. Wordlessly she turned to the hearth to rise a fire of dry seaweed and wrack and twigs.

'It's that Methuselah who was in the tavern,' said the fisherman, bending to loosen clothes. 'Go easy or you'll waken the children. There's a stink of beer off him.'

'Where would he get it, the unfortunate?'

'I think it's soldiers' drink. He drinking and good men being...'

'Hush!' the housewife said. She held the rushlight closer to the pallid, blue-veined face with its dank stringy beard, glistening with grains of sand. 'Look! he's trying to speak. Bring him near the fire!'

II

When Mr. Felton had drunk the last sweet drop of his morning coffee and savoured it with thin compressed lips, and when he had removed with precise finger-tips a crumb from the sleeve of his dressing-gown, he sighed lightly, arose and stood before the dining-room window through which the sunlight flowed immaculately. His wife looked over the rim of her lifted cup, and her pale-blue eyes blinked reflectively in the china pallor of her face. He stood with his back to her, and rubbed with his fore-finger the closely cropped greying hair on his wigless head. Calmly she noted his restless gestures. He began to pace in front of the window, his shadow coming and going across the polished table and her face. Occasionally he stopped to glance out into the garden where, at the far end of a parched lawn, espaliered pear trees and a mass of roses were warming under the sun. His thin nose, pointed chin and high forehead were sharp against the flawless light.

She put down her cup carefully. 'Robert,' she said, 'would you like your snuff-box?'

He waved a hand indefinitely but yet elegantly. 'No, dear, no. What's that?' he said. Brightly, he added, 'I am glad that Greaves has departed, that's all. A week's stay for himself and his mob was quite sufficient. Soldiers? Damn him, he was inventing trouble.'

'Why must we have all that again, Robert?'

'Yes! Yes! Yes!' The silken tone never left his voice. He faced the garden again and spoke to her with his head turned a little sideways. 'Do you know, dear, since Robert went into the army and Matilda married, I have never been quite, ah! quite settled?' He smacked his lips slightly. 'I'm not an old man...'

'Nor a young one, either, Robert.'

'And I have some ambitions left,' he continued with a touch of defiance. 'A stroke of good fortune, some work of value to, let us say, the government, in these times of trial and then, who knows?' He snapped his right finger and thumb. 'Who knows? I'm really a rare kind of magistrate for these parts, Maria.'

'The others are hardly gentlemen, are they?' she said sourly, closing her eyes against the strong morning. 'But aren't you comfortable?' She opened her eyes and whispered, tauntingly, 'Haven't you a good wife, too?'

He had returned to his pacing. 'Comfortable? Yes, Maria. The people, poor devils, are peaceful; that is, at present. My tenants pay their rents dutifully and there never has been any trouble about tithes. I think they are loyal. Their priest is, in any case! But sometimes, I regret I did not stand for parliament when... Besides, you always wished for a house in Dublin.'

'That was years ago,' she said, smiling meditatively. 'Do seat yourself, Robert, or take a stroll on the lawn. Don't you think we ought to visit a watering-place soon? I know you hate a removal.'

'Yes!' he murmured heedlessly. He paused with his back to the light and his face dark, and placing the tips of his fingers together as if he were about to pray, an act to which he was unaccustomed, he spoke rapidly: 'Do you recall that ludicrous young man who was here some time ago? The pedlar with the spectacles, the bouncing young gentleman with the grey eyes and the nice manners who paid you so many just compliments.'

'Oh! now, Robert.'

'Hume, wasn't it?'

'Tomás, at the tavern, insisted – privately of course – that Hume was – well, not quite an honest man.'

'But the letters of introduction?'

'In perfect order, my dear; and his conversation, which we found most diverting, was thoroughly loyal. – By the way, remind me this evening to send a messenger to Dungarvan. There may be some French liquors there for me. Only for this contraband, we should die of thirst in this Barbary. Thank heavens they do not infuse their republican sentiments into their wines and brandy. – What was I saying?'

He plucked with caressing fingers at his long saturnine face and allowed his heavy eyelids to droop against the sidelong rays of the sun.

'Mr. Hume,' she prompted. 'The French.'

'The French! Mr. Hume,' he repeated. 'My dear, I'm afraid I have suggested a false relationship. No matter.' He chuckled, looking down his nose at her. 'Well, Greaves, that savage, searched Hume's belongings at the tavern. Naturally I was present and I really feared he would discover something. But there was nothing except clothes, spectacles and the like. There wasn't a single scrap of paper nor a letter of any kind. Greaves did not see anything peculiar in that. Not a scrap! Greaves expected a nest of United men.'

'I thought,' said she, 'that the Government had dealt with that society. Go on, dear.'

'There was a poor begging fellow at the inquiry...'

'The blind man who had his clothes tied with rope? I heard they dealt with him most inhumanely.'

With a small gesture of impatience, he said, 'Such things happen. Despite his cringing he possessed a certain share of uncommon dignity. He, also, mentioned Hume at the inquiry. The strange character of the entire business is that only he and our sly Tomás had a word to say about the spectacle-pedlar. I met fishermen who, as Tomás is prepared to swear, drank with Mr. Hume, but they are equally prepared to swear, it seems, that Tomás is a liar. And the last time Tomás saw Hume was in the tavern-yard, shaking this blind old man's hand. Yes! Yes!'

'I can make neither head nor tail, Robert,' said she, rising from the table, 'of your insinuations.'

'I'm not sure that I can myself.' He smiled wryly. 'Mr. Hume was to return a week ago. He has not.' He pressed the palms of his hands together as if he were flattening creased paper. 'Mr. Hume and this beggar have something in common. I wonder if it is of any value,' he murmured. He turned with a swing, saying, 'I'm sure a stroll to the shore would clear my faculties, dear. Now, where did I leave my snuff-box?'

'I wish,' she said, sighing, 'that you would tell me these things when they happen. You make a secret and a burden of them.'

He patted her shoulder and with his dressing-gown billowing, hurried from the room to find his snuff.

III

Donnacha Ruadh, sitting with his back to the front wall of the fisherman's cabin, also soaked in the sun on that morning. He had, in the week, returned to the old passionless, almost pulse-less waiting for the last of his days. He settled grimly into his old way of living as though he were burrowing with his shoulders for a comfortable grave. On the Sunday, at Mass in the stone barn beyond the magistrate's house, he had knelt on the stone floor, leaning alone against a wall, mumbling his prayers and beating his breast, and at the Consecration when the Host was raised, he had wept, praying and pleading for forgetfulness of the things that had been done to him lest they should come between him and the final security of his soul. All he wanted was to stretch and be still and undisturbed.

At first the three children of the house had been in terror of him, scuttling to their mother away from the raw-rimmed empty eyes and from the greedily feeling hands that searched stone and grass and wood and the shape of features and the softness of the hair; but since one of the children had found his hat and stick where he had lost them on the road, they approached nearer and talked with him and tried to catch the meaning of the stories that he would start, and forget with a sigh.

'Once upon a time,' he would begin, 'there was a warrior in Ireland and his name was Fionn. He was a mighty hunter, and one day himself and the men of the Fianna were out hunting the deer on the slopes and they met a lady...' He would cease, and presently ask their names for the third or fourth time in the day, and after that he would ask: 'And what colour is your hair? Are you tall? How old are you? And what did your father take out of the sea yesterday? When did he take you out of the sea?'

Soon they walked with him as his eyes, and fed him and plucked his beard when he was in good humour. There was a great healing in their play and their talk, and the making of a great repose in the hearth of a house that did not spurn him. The night at the tavern sank in his mind and drifted up to trouble him only in dreams. He could be secluded in his own peace and there, once more, he could watch the immobile unchanging comforting past, and converse with the dead, his friends.

'Seán,' he said to the fisherman, 'you give me a place to lie and a bite to eat, and I pray that he'll not forget you and your own.'

He hardly said more to them of what he thought unless, carefully, they questioned him. It was the children he sent night and morning to the tavern, inquiring after Hume, and when they would come back with no message he would sit for a few minutes, restless with his fingers, and then, apparently, forget. The evening, when the light was soft as silver smoke and he could feel it like a chrism on his eyes, was the part of the day in which he seemed to flourish and to be rid altogether of furtive thoughts. He was not cantankerous then, nor were his few words gnarled like an ancient hawthorn bush. He was meek, tempered to alert serenity. He sat with them in their cabin and ate of the dried fish and the potatoes cooked over the fire of sticks, and he smacked his lips to the salt that coated everything, and when they had finished their meal, he would answer their questions about his youth and his schoolmastering and the fights there used to be against the landlords, and they would listen, finding the meaning that he intended them to find: if things were so evil in those far days, how much better were they not now? Sometimes when the scuffling night winds drove the smoke down into the cabin, he would choke and wheeze and ask the children to lead him down to the boat beached on the sand where he would sit, alone, always listening to the lapping waters, sometimes muttering, until time came for sleep.

'Why,' Seán inquired, 'do you be for ever asking after that gentleman, Hume?'

Donnacha answered gruffly: 'Once he was kind to me. Kindness is not as plentiful as an old man would like. I want to thank him.'

'I also drank with him,' said Seán. 'He was the strange

gentleman to be drinking with folk like us, like you and me. Wasn't he now? But they say they have different customs in the northern parts.

'And he said things that would go to our heart, and his talk was better than any of the old songs that only make men sad and weary. He spoke about...'

'I know,' Donnacha said abruptly. 'They were fine words.' He snatched in the air with a hand, closed his empty fist and chuckled. 'You couldn't catch the sense of them, no more than you could hold a fistful of air.'

'Some day, please God, they'll come true, his words, and we'll have our own.'

'We? Who are we?' Resignedly, Donnacha nodded. 'Who are we? Now, will you tell me, who are we? When I was young, Seán, there were men who could tell tales of the last battle fought in Ireland at Limerick town. That was more than a hundred years ago. It was, Seán! Well, we met defeat. We were made to serve the stranger. Friend, don't be telling a man of my years who we are.'

'Some day we'll be like the French. No! not like them. We'll...'

'There was a farmer I knew and he had a big wound, a hole in his shoulder. He got it in his shoulder. He got it in those wars. A hundred years ago, man. He got the wound from a ball on the walls.'

'Words like Hume's are better than...'

'Words! words! The years go over our heads and words are forgotten like the little winds that blew yesterday.'

'They'll blow up a fire one of these fine days.'

'And then,' said Donnacha, angrily, 'there won't be peace or ease any more for a man like me.'

He took his own words with him, like the repeated and remote talk of people in a dream, as he lay down beneath the small window of the cabin, and mumbled his moan of prayer while the household yawned and twisted and scratched itself to sleep. The years go over our heads and words are forgotten like the little winds that blew yesterday! Many times during the night, when he awoke from his intermittent sleep and snuffed and cleared his throat in the sultry air that reeked of fish and stagnant smoke and bodies, or when he reached for the mug that stood filled beside the wooded pail and sucked water noisily down his parched throat, his own lightless, despairing words sang back to him. The years go over our heads and here we lie and here we will ever lie in cabins and huts set on the reedy, unfruitful lowlands and the stony high places. It must have been always, always like that, even before he as an infant could distinguish the sun from the moon. How old was he? Back through all the years he receded, recalling forgotten marks: he smiled to himself at the honour men once gave to scholars and poets like himself; and again he smiled at the way a woman, his wife, regarded him with wrinkled amused eyes, as he argued learnedly with a priest. She was gone. The learning was falling to dust. The little winds that blew yesterday had taken everything. He was out of his time, estranged by his years, isolate. None now gave their hearts to learning in the ancient fashion and few composed verse worth a dram, and even the young could mouth out the English. Some things were up, some down: they had their dances and their wakes and their christenings; their priests were not hunted any more for money or for hate; their priests even had a share of respect and occasionally one of them would be invited to dine at the house of a gentleman whose forefathers, wolfish with the hungerings of apostasy, would gladly have dragged a priest to the killing. There was peace, indeed. But now, there were no leaders, no man of the old blood to go before the people, no rider mounted for the fighting and with the sword. In truth there was peace. Savouring the rankness of the decay of the people out of whom he was born, he groaned out in the night. Soon, there would be an end. Even he, the scholar and the poet, was losing count of the days that marked out the brief final time, days sinking imperceptibly like milestones in the grass and weeds at the edge of the highway.

He turned, lay on his side, pawed inside the breast of his shirt for the leather bag that contained his wealth, and assured thus, soon fell into a doze in spite of the odorous sweltering air.

IV

'I was selling lobsters to-day,' said Seán, 'to Felton's woman, and she told me the magistrate himself was in the garden waiting to have a word with me. The old bucko was out with a scissors, snipping roses, and after a deal of soft talk about the fishing and my family, he began to prate about yourself.'

'What was he saying?' Donnacha Ruadh asked eagerly. 'He was kind to me at the tavern.'

'He asked me about you. I told him you were a poet and he said he knew that.'

'A poet? My day is gone. Go on, Seán.'

'And I told him that your people lived up in the hills, and that you travelled the world over when you were young, and that now you wished to go home but you couldn't get a cart going northward.'

'And he listened to all that?'

'More than that. He said it was a shame to see a man of your learning – what was it he said? – a man of your accomplishments left homeless.'

'He's a fine gentleman.'

'He's a serpent,' Seán retorted. 'He asked me if I knew Mr. Hume, and before I could answer he said that Hume was an astonishing young gentleman. Those were the very English words he used. An astonishing young gentleman. Then he came back to yourself and says he, "I should like to meet this old poet. Could he come to my house to-morrow evening?" He really said that.'

'You're fooling me, Seán. What would a gentleman like Mr. Felton be doing with a man like me?'

'That's what I'd like to know,' Seán said slowly. 'But go if you please. I'll bring you. He has a soft voice. It goes over you like warm water. And he looks at you queerly like a fox peering out of a hole. Go if you like. I wouldn't.'

'I'll go.'

'I'm not fooling you,' said Seán.

V

Mr. Felton poured out a second glass of sherry for his visitor and continued to speak: 'You do not know, Mr. MacNamara how much pleasure your visit gives me. Seldom does one meet a scholar in these parts. No! I'm not flattering. I regret that I never learned your language when you tell me that our country possesses poets whose worth has not been guessed at by people like myself. I'm told you know Latin and Greek. I once knew a little Latin myself and small Greek but I feel, what shall I say? I feel abashed in the presence of a man of your attainments. Here I have a library – many of the books are in the Latin tongue and not a few of them belong to my son who had a brilliant course at Trinity College, of which you've heard, I'm sure – here I have a library – and I must confess that I seldom use it as I should. But you know how a man's life can be...' His speech sauntered on while he sat motionless in his chair, his elbows supported by the armrests, his hands clasped lightly together, his eyes noting even the quiver of a lip in the man who sat opposite, facing the evening light from the tall, uncurtained windows.

The light silvered the scant hair on the head and the combed beard, and it searched out the innumerable lines of the face, the droop of the gummy mouth, the calloused hands and broken finger-nails, and the patched, reefed and many-stained clothes. One foot had its upper split to a gape, and bare grimy toes showed. At first the man had sat up rigidly, warily, but the wine and even flow of talk had eased him into a slouch and now he rested, nodding, interrupting only with 'Do you say so, Mr. Felton?' or with 'Aye, sir, it is so.'

'I beg your pardon,' the magistrate apologised, 'for making a monopoly of the conversation. Please tell me of your travels on the Continent. Where were you?'

The head had sunken and the beard was crumpled in the folds of the coat. 'It was long ago, sir. Rome, sir, Rome in Italy.'

'The French are advancing through Italy at present, I believe.'

'I'm what people call a spoiled priest, Mr. Felton. I was in the college in Rome and then I left, and I was in Germany and I came home. Oh! I travelled. I was in the place they call Newfoundland. You see, Mr. Felton, a spoiled priest is not much good, they say. Not much good.' He emptied his glass, a few drops escaping down his chin on his beard, and pressed his lips together on the taste. The faintness of a wandering mind was already in the tone of his voice.

Laughing, Felton said, 'You disprove the rule. In truth you do, Mr. MacNamara.'

'I saw many lands,' Donnacha went on, 'and many faces.' He was talking then in a low monotone. The magistrate was obliged to lean forward but he could not hear distinctly what was said by the loose, hesitant mouth that smothered speech. He did perceive for a moment during which his dispassionate heart was stirred that this man carried more than the mere enfeebling burden of long years, and for the moment he felt a shadow, like doom, weighing upon him and shutting out the light falling on the brown carpet and the mahogany and on the papers and ink-stand on the table and annihilating the rose-scent that wreathed through the room from the quiet garden. This man was not one man, but thousands – a people. For a moment he felt the mood and then, rising and going to the table, he was himself again.

'Come, Mr. MacNamara,' said he, 'another glass.' But his voice was louder. 'Will you be staying for long in Bunmahon? I'm sorry that we did not meet before this day.'

The yellow-skinned face seemed to awaken to life. 'I'll be going, sir, as soon as I can get a cart or any kind of a lift. But before I go I have to meet an old friend.'

'I wonder,' said Felton, 'if your friend is mine also. Your good health, sir.'

They clinked glasses. Felton was smiling.

'He is then, sir. Mr. Hume it is. This is grand drinking, sir.'

'Thank you. I see you like good wine. Of course, Mr. Hume. Why, he is a friend of mine.'

'Well, I have a message for him, but if he doesn't come back before I go, he'll do without it.'

'Seán tells me that you are going north. I should like to help you, Mr. McNamara, if I may? Is the message for our friend very important? Perhaps, if you gave me the opportunity...'

'Thank you, sir. I don't know if it was important. I'm keeping it for him and I'd rather wait.'

'To be sure. To be sure. But please remember that I'm still willing to do all... Here comes Seán to take you home.' Felton stood closer and taking the old man's right hand shook it, saying, 'I sincerely hope we'll meet again shortly. Now, this is your stick and this is your hat. This way, now. Do visit me again. Say in three or four days. We'll go out by the garden-gate. Good evening. Good evening. Don't forget what I said, now. Eh!'

When Felton returned to the library he stood to contemplate the chair on which the visitor had sat before the window. He was still standing there, fingering his chin, as his wife entered, sniffing, and fanning the air with her hands.

'Thank heavens,' she said, 'he's gone. Why didn't you bring him into the garden.'

'I think, Maria,' he said meditatively, 'I was right.' She was removing the glasses from the table. 'The vain old fool... But still, Maria...' He rubbed his forehead as though to enliven slow thoughts. 'Do you recall,' said he, 'the very decrepit Jew we once met in France when times were happier in that country? Le Havre, wasn't it? He was like the last survivor of his race, the old wandering creature of the legends. What am I saying?'

VI

On the next day Mrs. Felton's maidservant called to one of the fisherman's children from the road. She had a bundle. It was a present from her mistress, with compliments, to Mr.

MacNamara. There was no other message. The bundle contained a long frieze coat that had been worn but little.

'Now, Mr. MacNamara,' Seán jeered, fumbling for the English in the midst of the Irish, 'do you see what it is to be a friend of a gentleman? But be wary. Since you went there, every second word out of your mouth is about the magistrate and what you said to him.'

'It'll be my Sunday coat,' said Donnacha. 'Help me, will ye, till I fit it on. Help me.' He began to untie and unbutton his old coat and when he had one arm out of it, he paused, with his head sideways, and said, 'Be careful of this old coat. It'll do me a while yet. Here, put it at my feet, so as I'll know where it is.' He put on the new coat which fitted well enough and they buttoned it for him and pulled it down on the shoulders and guided the groping hands to the deep side-pockets. 'It's the best of stuff,' he boasted. 'I'm a made man. I'll go home like a real gentleman. Now, Seán, my man, what did I tell you? Did I utter a word of a lie? Isn't Mr. Felton a gentleman and isn't he my friend? Admit it, you ruffian.' He felt around him anxiously with his feet and of a sudden ceased his cackling. He grasped at the air around him and burst out with, 'Where's my old coat? Come here with it. Give me my coat. I want my coat. I want to put it on. You robbers. Give me that coat.'

'He's in earnest,' said the housewife.

They gave him his coat which he snatched and put on after many efforts. When he had it tied once more he patted the pockets with their tattered flaps.

'You must have treasure there,' Seán said, but he got no answer for the old man was sulking.

On the day before the second visit Seán asked boldly, 'What are you going to talk about with Mr. Felton? What would he be wanting with you?'

'That's something, son, that myself and the magistrate know best. I don't mean any offence. Mr. Felton, as you know, has a library and we'll be talking about the books. We will. And he'll give me wine. That's all.'

'I don't believe a word of it,' Seán replied. Then he had to skip back, for the old man was up, swinging the stick, his mouth working to frame some terrible curse, but the only sound that came was a choked, breathless bellow. Immediately, calling the housewife, Seán walked away, shaken by the outburst. It took the wife many minutes to pacify Donnacha Ruadh who, throwing his stick aside, sat pale and quivering as from a cold and whispering into the fire that there was no kindness at all left in the world for an old man. That evening the children did not go near him.

In the night they heard him whispering still and wishing that he were among his own. In the night, too, the wind changed and blew chill from the mountains where he desired to go.

VII

There was a wood-fire in the magistrate's library, for the day after the storm was like a blast of late November: windy, damp and unseasonably cold. The tail of the wind that had growled down from the mountains lashed across the sky the flying tatters of the rain-clouds. The distant beach was deep in weed torn from the rocks and the sea-bed. It was rumoured that, beyond Dungarvan, two Brittany fishing-boats had been battered to pieces against one arm of a cove but no one knew whether any souls had been lost. They were sure that the early storm was a sign of a bad, bitter winter.

Mr. Felton was languid in his chair before the fire. He begged to be excused if he appeared to be out of sorts because, as he explained, the wind had lifted a few slates on the lee-side of the house during the night and rain had come through, and the disturbance had deprived him of his full sleep. 'Besides,' he said, jabbing with a poker at the fire, 'the storm cleaned all the young fruit from my trees. My plums are mere pulp on the ground, and as for my roses, I hardly dare look at their sad state. Pray excuse me, Mr. MacNamara, if I seem lacking as a host.'

While he was saying these things, Donnacha Ruadh, his head hot and stuffy for want of sleep, was recalling what the wind had done to Seán the fisherman's house. It was the housewife who had screamed them all from rest and she cried that the roof was letting in the rain in torrents. Seán ran out, looking first to the boat, and through the open door they heard the ravening of sea battering against wind, and in the fury the voices of the woman and her children were like the sighing and keening of flocking birds. Rain puddled the mud-floor and made the straw sodden and clothes damp. No one could sleep then, and there was no time for an old man's sulks. The household could only wait, open-eyed for the morning. One of the children whimpered when a stick from the roof fell upon its face, and from the words that followed between the housewife and Seán, Donnacha Ruadh understood that the woman was with child.

Mr. Felton's roses had been destroyed, and Mr. Felton was a gentleman, besides being a magistrate. 'I'm sorry for your trouble,' said Donnacha Ruadh. 'I excuse you, sir.'

'What was that you said?'

The question was snapped out, but almost instantly the tone changed to the customary suave wheedle.

'Mr. MacNamara, I have good news for you, that is, if you care to receive it as such. I am sending a man with a cart to a friend of mine with some goods; Mr. Dundee of Lacken, north of Kilmacthomas, you know. A fine country seat! If you wish to travel with my carter, he might be persuaded to go further to your destination. I could say a few words to him. He will be carrying...'

'Anything from France, sir?'

'Who told you? Dammit, I wish those prying fishermen would attend to their own affairs. It's no concern...'

'I beg your pardon, Mr. Felton. I really meant no harm, your honour. Honest to God, sir...'

Felton relaxed again and remained silent for a minute during which Donnacha Ruadh listened anxiously for the low, caressing speech that came at last. 'Well, my friend, do you wish to go? I'll not be offended if you say no.'

'Do you mind, sir, if I ask you when?'

'To-morrow. Early, too, I believe.'

'But, Mr. Felton, I have to do something. I wouldn't be an honest man if I backed out of it. I was paid, sir, in truth. The gentleman with the spectacles gave me a whole sovereign. On my honour, Mr. Felton.'

'Dear! dear! why not leave the message with a friend? I should be only too glad to help you, but then, perhaps you don't trust me. Perhaps...' Felton leaned forward and laid a hand on the old man's arm.

'Oh! I do trust you, sir. Indeed I trust you more than anyone in all Bunmahon. Wasn't it yourself put in a good word for me at the tavern? Wasn't it your own self gave me this grand coat I'm wearing?'

'That,' said the magistrate lazily, 'was nothing. A kind thought of Mrs. Felton's. As I was saying, if you put your trust in me as a keeper of your message, you'll not be disappointed. After all, I, too, have a friendly interest in Mr. Hume. He is a quaint character in spite of his youth, and I believe him to be very clever in spite of his modesty. What is your opinion, Mr. MacNamara? You have known more of the world than I have.'

He spoke so quietly and without a quiver of excitement that

his voice never rose above a level insinuating murmur, like a lullaby when the child is almost captured by sleep; and all the while his eyes, lively and sharp, never withdrew their gaze from the bearded troubled face.

'He is,' said Donnacha Ruadh, agreeing heartily, 'he is a clever man, just as you say, sir. But what I can't make out is how he'll find the message if I give it into your care?'

Felton was sitting up, alert. 'Leave that to me. I'll have it sent to him as soon as he returns to the tavern. The very instant! His business, I'm sure, has taken him farther afield than he anticipated. Indeed, now that I recall it, he did mention a meeting with a friend or client in Carrick or thereabouts. Well, what is the message? Do I need pen and paper?'

'It's a packet, sir.'

The magistrate took out his snuff-box, tapped it with shaking fingers, snuffed, and producing a handkerchief, blew his nose loudly. 'A packet?' said he, 'a packet? Now, now!'

'Letters or papers. I have it here. Look, sir, here it is. I never left it from me the whole time. I changed it to this gallant coat because people are curious. I don't know what's in it and it's not my business.'

'Nor mine, Mr. MacNamara. Nor mine,' Felton replied, arising and removing the packet gently from the two wrinkled hands that, for a second, clasped it tightly and then reluctantly let it go. 'Here,' continued the magistrate, striding across the room, 'is a drawer with an excellent lock. I preserve my own papers in this drawer.' He hummed a tune as he jingled keys and finally he slammed home a drawer and clicked a lock. 'There now. Safe and sound. Now, sir, what will you drink? I must be leaving you soon to settle a little matter with the carter for to-morrow. Sherry again? Excellent! You have a fine royal taste, Mr. MacNamara.'

He filled one glass, placed it in Donnacha's hands and stood tapping his fingers impatiently on his pointed chin as if it were the lid of his snuff-box. In his daydream he little heeded the halting, throaty dribble of words that came from the figure in the chair before the fire, and only when the glass had been drained did he attend again. He opened the door of the room, called for a maidservant and told her to help Mr. MacNamara to the road and, if needs be, home.

Saying good-bye mechanically and reaching out for what he could not find, Donnacha Ruadh allowed himself to be guided out by the silent girl. For one instant the notion of being dismissed like a beggar troubled him, but it was dispelled by the procession of images that the farewell of the magistrate summoned up. 'A pleasant journey to-morrow,' Felton had said, 'and a happy home-coming.' What more could a man, bending his gaze to find his couch in the clay, ask of the whole world? A happy home-coming! Familiar hands and familiar laughter were all about him, and he was being led to a house where, without enemies and with his own kin, he could sit at ease like a prince and be called master and be heeded as a man of worth.

'Girl,' said he on the road to the maidservant, 'I tell you they'll open their arms.'

The magistrate had hardly waited till he was gone. He had taken the packet from the drawer, torn the strip that bound it and unloosed on the table a bundle of stiffly folded papers. He unfolded them, tearing their edges slightly in his haste. Over at the window in the evening light, he scanned them, throwing on the floor some letters, too personal to be of much use, addressed from northern towns and the capital. At last he discovered something like what he sought in a long sheet of listed names and memoranda. His thin lips were chalky.

'Maria,' he shouted, 'Maria, come here. I knew it. There's no doubt of it. Maria, come here. I knew it. There's no doubt of it. Maria, Greaves was fooled. But not me. Maria, that spectacle-seller, he's one of them.'

VIII

The light cart rocked and jolted northward along the narrow, rutted road. Sometimes the driver walked, sometimes he sat with his feet dangling; and he paid as much heed to the countless stones on the track as he did to the man who sat facing back, wedged between a box and a small cask on the floor of the car, with his stick and his bundle on his knees and his high-crowned hat bobbing to the springless motion. The weather was holding up, and once they were down behind the first line of hills in the shelter of a valley where the sea-wind was felt no more and the smoke of fires could be sniffed on the air, the heat was heavy and sweet like a drug. There the people were reaping.

Torpid, his body jiggling from the hips, Donnacha Ruadh sat on the damp straw. His back was against the box and his feet were pressed flat against the tailboard. Long ago, in the morning, he had given up trying to talk to the carter, and with the silence, the continuous shaking and the grinding of the wheels, he had fallen into a dull doze. The day passed in a blear of sound and of changing shadows and bands of vague light. The sun had beaten first upon his face; now it burned at the back of his head. Occasionally, from the heat, he slumbered in faintness to be awakened when the cart swayed violently or when the carter shouted, but despite disturbance he seldom deserted the secret place inside him in which he resided, shut off from the world and lit by an unflickering joy. It was like a room wherein, high and above the hub-bub of the brawling street and removed from the wearying traffic of time, a man draws the bow across a beloved fiddle in tune to his heart's content till his eyes are troubled no more and he is sure of his immortality.

The sun swung down its heat; the cart shook his breath; his right knee, bruised where he had knocked it against the wheel on mounting the cart, smarted saltily; but all these things were nothing, nothing at all: was he not going towards his own? In his mind he acted what would happen at the end of the journey; and as the creatures moved and spoke according to his will in the bright light he cast upon them, the outer world which he could not fashion to his desire reminded him that it was there by the ceaseless turning of the wheels, the click-clack of the hoofs, the splashing through a stream that scoured across the road, and the coolness and dovelike cooing of wayside trees and groves that responded to the slightest whim of the brooding air. At midday the carter pulled up in a village and bought himself a mug of beer and bread, but Donnacha remained in the cart in the shade of a wall, the flies buzzing on his twitching face; and thus, patiently, he worked at his dream of crossing the threshold of his own folk. First he would stay in Knockanee with his son and his son's children and after that, before they could grow tired of him and his crotchety ways and when he felt that another winter would bring the end, he would take to the road for the last time and go down beyond Kilmacthomas, to where his daughter and her man were living on a fine little farm with a houseful, and in the comfort of that place he could lie waiting without fear. It was best to be in the house of a woman, in a daughter's house, when the end was on you, because a woman came nearer to you with comforting when the last terror tried to topple you from your balance. He wouldn't be any expense to her either, alive or dead, for he could live on as little as a bird, and his wake and funeral could be paid for out of his own purse. The creatures of his day-dream moved as he bade them. He was very happy.

In the evening while he was trying to fit a few lines of verse together, his mind being alert in the coolness that had a touch of autumnal frost in it, the cart rolled into the yard at the rere of Lacken House.

'Here, out of that, you,' the carter said. 'Give me the bundle. Lean on my shoulder.' He lifted Donnacha from the cart, set him on his stiff yielding feet, steadied him and put the bundle under his arm.

'Well,' said a woman-servant in English, 'what can I do for you?'

'Nothing! This is from Mr. Felton to Mr. Dundee. Here is a letter for your master. Hurry up, woman.'

The carter began unloading the boxes and the little cask. Donnacha walked a few steps till his stick scraped a wall which he leaned against.

'Will you take me,' he said, 'the rest of the way to-night?' He knew his voice was too faint to be heard.

He wished he could speak at that minute like the hearty man who came out on quick feet into the yard. 'So you are from Mr. Felton,' said this man. 'Well, you must stay here for the night. Put the mare in the first empty stable you can find. I'll send one of the boys to look after her. Annie, give this man a good meal. There's cider for you if you care to have it.'

'Thank you,' the carter answered. 'Thank you kindly. Will I carry the boxes in, Mr. Dundee?'

'Will you take me on the rest of the way to-night?'

'Yes! Put the boxes in the kitchen. Take the cask with you, Annie.'

'Will you take me, do you hear? Will you bring me? Will you...'

'Who is this man?' asked Dundee.

'I don't know, sir,' said the carter.

'Oh, well, Annie, give him something to eat.'

Hastily tapping his way towards the voices, Donnacha said, 'He's to bring me home, Mr. Dundee.' He whined, 'My friend, Mr. Felton, said so. On my honour, Mr. Dundee.'

'Your friend!' Dundee exclaimed.

'In troth,' said the carter, 'the magistrate said nothing of the kind.'

'Nor did he write it,' Dundee added reflectively. 'Who are you, my man? Oh! dammit. Annie, give him something to keep him quiet. Let him settle his dispute with Felton's man.' Then, the quick footsteps died away into the house.

'Old man,' said the woman, 'stay where you stand. I'll attend

46

to you when I get time.'

'Please, miss, you have a kind manner. Please, miss, listen to me. Mr. Felton said...'

'You're a liar,' the carter interrupted.

'Miss, listen. I came all the way here to get to Knockanee to my people.'

'Knockanee?' the woman replied in Irish, her voice hard. 'They pay rent there to the master. The hill over there it is. Who are you?'

'I'm Donnacha Mac Conmara and I have a young son there, married, with a family. Won't you ask the man to give me a lift, miss?'

'There's a Donnacha Mac Conmara living in Knockanee but he's not young, either himself or his wife. The daughter married away and one son is... don't be bothering me anyway.'

'Don't heed him,' said the carter. 'He's daft. Come on, my fine woman, and get me a bit.' The woman squealed as the carter caught her under the arm and pushed her towards the kitchen door.

Donnacha sidled back to the wall. He turned his head this way and that like a dog searching a bare floor. He stooped and sank slowly to the ground, feeling the dry tiny snapping of his legjoints, and there he sat to wait for his bite of food. His face was screwed up as he strove to make out how it was that he could have forgotten the age of his own son. He hissed through softly pursed lips and shook his head when the question baffled him. Of the magistrate or the spectacle-seller or even of the people in the house, he was not thinking at all, but of the kind of people who bore his own name on the hill beyond the yard. The smell of wood-smoke and of baking potatoes was a tang on the air. There would be frost.

CHAPTER III

Fire from France

I

A stream scored the hollow between the two slopes on which the scattered houses and cabins of Knockanee stood. In the summer the water, always clear and never too wide for a man to leap, dwindled to a trickle that bubbled to itself as it ventured among mossy stones and beneath the cart-track roughly bridged, for a way down to the valley. Down there the well-nourished Lacken river bore it through the richer fields around Lacken House. In the winter it became proud and loud and garrulous with the drainings of the hills.

There was one stone house with glass in its window and with a slated roof that had been built in the earlier days for the herdsman of the baronet who once owned Lacken. The rest of the houses were mud-walled, thatched, small, the windows unglazed, their whole appearance as mottled and dun as the clay from which they had been moulded. There were no trees, only clumps of furze higher up where the sheep grazed and a few gnarled thorns on which berries were ripening like little glowing lamps.

The house of Donnacha, son of Donnacha Ruadh Mac Conmara, was farthest up the stream, beside the path that straggled up over the hills across a sodden, boggy pass. It faced the southwest. Behind it, the slope warded off the villainous winds of the heavens, and all that a man could grumble about was that the sough of the breezes, coming far across the crumpled land from the sea, never ceased and that when the skies were thick the rain beat straight in the door.

But, in still cloudless weather, the sunshine was cordial on the front wall.

II

There would not be many more days of sitting before the door in the sunshine with the stream bubbling quietly and little noises mounting up from the road far down in the valley. The breaking of the weather had put a nip, like a hidden poison, in the morn-

48

ings when old muscles and sinews twinged in protest. And so, in the evenings, when the hill-shadows crept coldly across the tiny fields, and mists, yellowish to the moon and opaque, uprose along the lowlands and the broad stubble fields and submerged the trees and groves and drenched the wind-blown orchards, Donnacha Ruadh would rise from his seat before the wall and go indoors to his stool beside the fire. There he would await the neighbours, old men mostly, who would lament the terrible changes that had come over the elements since they were boys, and then, straining to recall fine impossible summers of milk and honey, they would argue themselves hoarse, raising a hub-bub in the narrow house, or sink to silence in an attempt to comprehend what it was the decrepit poet uttered in his tan-trums; and it was a deep fear-inhabited silence he could force on their lips when he, in disconnected phrases, recalled the iron winter of seventeen-forty when men died of hunger, rooting at the earth they could not break.

'They're only boys; that's what they are, lads,' said he on one of those nights after they had gone and he was sipping his warm milk. 'They remember nothing. Heads like bad cabbage they have.'

'They're company anyway,' the son answered, 'if you don't put the run on them. Since the children went, there doesn't be much stirring in this house. Hurry up there and be making for bed. I'll go out and see if everything is right for the night.'

The housewife knelt down beside the fire to blow on the embers over which a pot of oatmeal simmered stickily. She blew and straightened up with a sigh beside Donnacha Ruadh.

'Tell me, daughter,' he asked, 'what does my son look like now? I heard him saying that yourself and himself were well on in years. He was always full of old man's guff.'

She laughed softly and eerily. 'He's the same son of yours,' she said shortly. 'Ugly, strong, abrupt. They tell me he's a good farmer. He reared his family. He wears a fine coat of a Sunday and shaves his face. There now.'

'There now,' he repeated.

'We're happy enough in Knockanee. I wouldn't like to leave it. The landlord's a good man. The people are the best of neigh-bours.'

'I remember,' said he, nodding solemnly, 'I remember when he took you from your mother in Slieve Gua, Eibhlín. You were as plump then as...'

'The house here had children in it since. They didn't see much of their grandfather, who was wandering the roads of Munster and the Decies. I wish I knew how it fares now with my fine sons. We're alone, we are so.'

Impulsively he put out his hand and touched her head and then, what he sought, her face. She did not shrink. She submitted, still on her knees, to the questing thin cold fingers that circled her eyes and traversed her cheeks and delayed at the deep corners of her mouth so that she was conscious of her face as of a mask, and it was only when he removed his hand that she shivered, and covered her shoulders with a tug at her shawl. With her eyes fixed on the fire, but seeing only a red blur, she stood up.

'Daughter,' said Donnacha Ruadh, 'that's the woman's share. Aye, you're alone.'

'I hope I bear it well.'

The husband came in, leaned over the fire for a moment with his palms outstretched to the heat, and then stooping, began to untie his boots. Eibhlín went to the other end of the house, unbuttoned her bodice, and then as if recalling something, knelt with her face to the wall.

'There'll be frost on the fields in the morning,' the son remarked.

'Tell me,' the father inquired in a whisper, 'do you ever have a gathering in the house at all? With fiddle-music and a drop to drink? Something to raise the heart?'

'No! Do you think we're rich. It'll be tight enough to pay the rent next Michaelmas.' The son bit on the words.

'Now, wouldn't you like to have a gathering, son? There'll be no expense in the wide world on you. I don't mean a dance with meat to eat. Just your nearest neighbours and ourselves and a fiddler.'

'Even that, no.'

'But I'll pay, son. It'll be a change for Eibhlín and yourself. I'll pay. Maybe it'll be my last gathering.'

'And where would you get the money, you that couldn't give a few pence to the carman to bring you here?'

'Ah!' said Donnacha Ruadh, leaning closer and shaking his head assuringly, 'I have a little, a little.'

'You're cracked. Go to bed and don't be talking foolish.'

'I'm not talking foolish. Don't answer me back. We'll have a good night here on this floor and that's enough of it. But look, son, how much rent do you owe?'

'Four pounds ten for the half-year. I can get it. I have three pigs fattening for a start and Mr. Dundee will be giving me work and that's another way of paying him. But wouldn't it answer you better to keep your own few pence for the day...'

'For the day of my funeral. Go on. Tell me my business. Who'll be dead? Whose funeral will it be? Here, give me a hand to bed.'

III

Eibhlín had swept the floor, banked up the fire and set the stools in readiness alongside the walls, and on the table in the corner she had put the drink, genteel drink like ale in a little keg, a cheap wine that Mr. Dundee's housekeeper had sold her at a profit, a small bottle with a few inches of brandy in it, and the harsh poteen in a jug. She had on her best and only Sunday dress with its flounced sleeves and lace collar. The old man sat beside the door welcoming, lifting his voice in spite of her pleas, for his attempt to be boisterously jovial was pitiable.

The women pulled their stools closer to the fire and whispered under the shelter of their hands and shawls and looked sideways at one another as they drank from the cups and mugs. The men sat on the floor or on their hunkers, drank, muttered, and were mostly dumb. The night wind cut across the floor. One of the women complained and the door was shut. The clatter of the latch drove away all the talk.

'Where's that fiddler?' Donnacha Ruadh asked. He felt warm. The brandy glowed in his stomach. 'Will you strike up a tune, man? This isn't my wake.'

The fiddler lifted the fiddle and with his hat tilted over his eyes began to play, first aimlessly, and then he wandered from tune to tune, playing a scrap of this and that, love-songs, lamentations for the dead, a song about a seaman who left women across the seas, the Munster Warsong with its throb and smash of sound, and songs about meeting a fair lady early in the morning and she walking alone, lovely, full-breasted and disconsolate. He played unheeded. They knew his tunes too well. Soon they were all talking loudly about the affairs of the parish, the priest, Mr. Dundee, the woman who had a child and no husband, and about the harvest that was almost completely in. Beside Donnacha Ruadh, two men became heated in an argument about the chance there was of the French coming some day to Ireland, and the older of the two men denounced the French, saying that king-killers and priest-killers could keep their help for all he cared. 'My God, man,' said he, 'don't I remember the time that

51

the students were driven back to Ireland from the colleges and they had the queer stories to tell about the mobs galloping around the streets and the blood running as deep as your ankle in the gutters. As deep as your knee, man. The French have no religion at all. Don't be talking to me, man. Wait till you grow up.' – 'Maybe it would do no harm to let some of it run here as deep as my knee.' – 'I'd like to see yourself then, begod. You'd be far away.' – And so on, ranting at one another, they rattled out words that were lost in the gabble through which the fiddle-notes meandered, lost, broken and infinitely forlorn.

A string of notes, a bar from a Jacobite song, were heard by Donnacha Ruadh and they wrought upon him so that, recalling at the same time the features and the proud bearing of the poet, long dead, who had made the song, meditating on the house that this poet had lived in and on the poets who used to foregather there and had been swept away by death, leaving himself like a stranded hulk between the land and the sea, he was filled with regret for the time that had ended. There would be no more gatherings of poets to make songs, only gatherings of windy, blustering, wordy boors. Men of the old kind had died out, and as the priest said in a sermon, let the dead bury the dead. But the regret hurt him like a great hunger. And drawing his stool towards the two arguing men whose talk he had hardly heard, he said fiercely, 'You don't know what you're talking about, either of you.' He was vehement. Silence spread out from him. His son bent over him, begging him not to shout thus and not to shame the house in the eyes of the people, but he cast off the hand that gripped his shoulder. 'You don't know a word on God's earth of what you're saying. Aye, we had a chance once when Charles the Prince fought in Scotland. And we had chances before that. I met men who fought at Limerick with Sarsfield that went to France, and when I was young there were old men who could tell of Cromwell. Why didn't we have victory then?' He beat the clay floor with his stick and his throat piped shrilly and his lips were flecked with bubbled drool. 'I'll tell you why. I'll tell you why we're the servants. I'll tell you why we're only dirt on the lands of the men who... I'll tell you.' But he didn't. He couldn't. The reason seemed to slip down in a gap in his mind whenever he had it almost in his grasp. He relapsed into a defeated croaking.

'Maybe something will happen soon.' It came from one of the men beside him.

'Hold your tongue,' said the son, Donnacha. 'You'll only set him off worse.'

'Whisht,' women whispered. 'Let him be.'

'No,' said Donnacha Ruadh, lifting his voice once more. 'I'll tell you what'll happen. The first move you make, if the French set foot in Ireland, will be the cause of destruction and burning and hanging and murder. They murdered the Christian man God put over them and they murdered the priests. Why can't you shut your mouths?' He pleaded, almost sobbing. 'Why can't you be content? I know. But nobody will listen to me. They'll come, the soldiers, and burn you out of Knockanee and they'll leave you homeless.'

'God between us and all harm!' It was a crone who spoke, piercingly shrill, a woman renowned for lore in herbs and healing, and amidst the other women she in her bundled clothes was like a dwarf, for age had dried her small and wizened features to thin, edged bone. 'May your words never come true,' she cried. She pulled her shawl's hood over her face as though a cold hungry wind were to be warded off, and out of the little shadowy cavern the shawl made around her firelit eyes, she mouthed gummily on a rigmarole of ancient words to forestall evil. Only one woman of all the company, the crone's daughter-in-law, seemed to catch a hint of the meaning and she, in the same tone as she would use in drawing down the Holy Name against the hurtling terror of the dead, spoke out, 'Let it come when it comes. Hold your peace, mother.'

IV

On Michaelmas Day, a Thursday, a man went down from every house in Knockanee to pay his rent at Lacken House. The men who had worked in Mr. Dundee's fields during the harvest carried their tally-sticks on which the work-days were notched, for Mr. Dundee was not a man to do away with the old custom of keeping accounts. Donnacha carried his tally and two pounds and some odd shillings, and he would carry nothing away except, as he expected, a reprimand for falling short.

Dundee sat behind a table in the stone barn where apples, potatoes, meal and honey were stored at the back of the house. He sat with his surcoat buttoned around his stout muscular body and affably named out the people to come, who stood about the door under the sidling brown and yellow mottled leaves from the trees sheltering the yard. While waiting for their turn to go to the table, they conversed in groups or lounged against walls and carts, scrutinizing and remarking the number of windows, chimneys and doors of the house they had seen so often before and wherein few of them had set foot farther than the kitchen. Out of respect they had on their good clothes, their knee breeches with grey or black woollen socks, heavy-soled shoes tied with thongs, long-tailed coats, thick rough shirts and coloured cravats, high-topped and low-crowned hats. Three or four men who farmed in the rich land of the valley wore corduroy and brass-buttoned waistcoats and these men stood apart.

'Before I begin,' Dundee said slowly in English, 'before I begin to forget it, I want to give fair warning.' The door was darkened with tenants. 'Mr. Loughlin, your priest, may have spoken to you already on this matter, but it's worth repeating. There are rumours flying about. They say that some men, strangers, are moving about the country, attempting to band poor misguided young men into some kind of society. And there's much talk of the French at the same time. Now let every one here know that I'll not stand for anything of the kind on my estate. Continue to behave like the honest decent people you are, whether you be at home or at a fair in a town. Do you understand?'

'We do, your honour.'

'Every word, sir.'

'True for you, Mr. Dundee.'

'We'll not fail you, your honour.'

'That's good. If I find any man... you understand me. I'd prefer not to have a visit from the military or our yeomen. They will not be so gentle. Now, let us continue with our business; and as is customary, every man who satisfies me in his account will find his half-pint of ale at the kitchen window. Now, you first.'

Donnacha returned home sullen. His father was by the fire, petting and pussing a scrawny cat.

'Well,' said the son in Irish, 'I got no ale.'

'Was he hard?'

'I must pay all I owe and what's to come as well by New Year's Day.'

'We'll have to sell the pigs,' Eibhlín cut in coolly, 'and they not ready nor the prices fair.'

'Devil a much my father cares,' the son muttered bitterly. 'Buying drink, I ask you, for the old fools and gossips of the townland, and now they're laughing at him for trying to ape the gentlemen with the fat purses.'

54

'Are you certain, son,' the father asked, 'that you can't pay it?'

'You couldn't stir a hand to help me anyway.'

'I'm only inquiring, son. Don't shout at me.'

'Oh! leave me alone. What has a man like you save words and learning and grief that they'll put down with you in the grave.'

'Aye! What has a man like me?'

V

On Sunday after reading the Gospel, Father Loughlin turned from the altar towards his people who stood close together on the flagged and unfurnished floor. Placing his hands beneath the threadbare chasuble either to shield them from the crisp cold air or to hide the nervous way the fingers of his two hands forked together, he began to preach on St. Michael, war-lord of the angelic hosts. While he preached, familiarly and with lumbering emphasis, his fluffy white eyebrows wriggled oddly.

St. Michael, he said, shrugging his shoulders, would always be leading his hosts against the armies of evil, and the battle wasn't any the less terrible because it was unheard and unseen by men's ears and eyes. Some people, he went on with gentle and affected scorn, thought that the battle was being waged when kings were being put to death and when blood was being spilt in torrents in the ruined streets and on the burnt fields. Maybe it was like that, but an old proverb said that the evil deed went back to a remote time, and the true battle between Saint Michael and Lucifer began long before men were made, in whose hearts and souls the battle was to-day.

Intently the congregation stared at him, their eyes puckered up as if by peering through the gloom they could see his words like trees or sails far away in a mist.

The slight movement they made all together, the little uplift of the heads, showed that the rest of the sermon went nearer to their minds. Donnacha Ruadh, supporting himself against the stone wall, felt the tremor of the people.

Now, the priest added, I wish to talk to you about the bad and evil doctrines that are being sown among you by men who would bring confusion on the people of the earth by going against government and law and order. We aren't escaping. Indeed we're not. Strange men are ferreting around the countryside, pretending they're on honest business, but all the while they're spreading false beliefs and putting false hope into the hearts of the fools that listen. Only last week one of them was caught in Youghal, and they say that he'll be punished for high treason, and you know what the punishment is, my people. Now, my children – and he paused, swaying his grey head and the words came haltingly from him – now, I'll say no more. I know our lot seems hard sometimes and it's easy to find promise of relief in every new word the wind carries, but be at peace, my people, because the great ones of this earth pass. The great ones pass.

He wheeled to the altar and with his hands flat upon the white cloth, remained for a moment contemplating the candle flame.

'He didn't say all he meant,' someone whispered.

'The great ones pass,' went among them like a breeze through the leaves of a tree.

Donnacha Ruadh, smiling, was thinking that all he had tried to say to people who would not heed him, had been said by the priest.

VI

'There was a time,' said Donnacha Ruadh, after long weeks spent in and about the house which had only a casual visitor now and again, 'there was a time when people came in droves by night to wherever I was with men of my kind. They could find delight in learning in those days and pay respect where it was due. Why wouldn't they? I and men of my kind took pride in it and boasted of it justly. Why wouldn't we ourselves. Not every man knew Virgil almost by heart as I do, as I did before age shook me; and not every man could follow Odysseus across the strange enemy seas and the foreign lands; and not every man knew the old books of Ireland, or the stories that men told and wrote down about Deirdre and Oisin and Fionn and the dead kings and lords. Why does a man become stale for making verse, stale and dry and crumbling like bread that has no sap in it? You will answer me it is because he gets old. But why does he get old?'

The son and Eibhlín listened patiently, amazed by such a flow of speech as they had not heard from him since the old days.

'People come no more to where I sit.

'I made the epitaph of a fine man, a holy man who could be merry and he was Tadhg Gaolach. They sing the hymns he made now. He's gone. No man will be left to make a line for my name or to mourn me. And I, I am breaking like a story in a forgetful mind; breaking; broken I am.

'In truth I know how good it is to be with my own flesh and

56

blood during these last years when the world changes so greatly that I can't recognise the face of it. I can sit at a hearth without feeling I'm being let sit there because I look like a beggar-man, and I can eat a bite without wondering if I'll get no bit to-morrow nor a sup, and I can talk to you without fear of being commanded to hold my tongue.'

Thinking he had finished and awaited an answer of some kind, the couple spoke; the son saying that they were always glad to have him under the same roof, the housewife adding that it was always so; but he did not hear them. His head was sideways. They hearkened to discover what he heard. He was sunken deep in stillness to catch the ceaseless sifting fall of time that, inaudible and persistent like the snow which would soon descend upon the land, enshrouded him with what he preserved memorially of his living, his youth and its pride, his travels, his harvest of praise for songs, his wife and her quiet loving, and all that had given laughter to his soul. Before him then, the engulfing jaws of the grave were as nothing.

VII

It cut down thinly, aslant and hard, one night after the frost and a few days before Christmas Eve. The frozen dry ground took it churlishly and let it pile up without any underthaw in drifts in the hollows of the hillside and in deep masses in the bed of the frozen, dribbling stream.

'Son,' said Donnacha Ruadh, 'take me outside.'

The son led him by the arm.

All the grey sky was sliding downward in taut lines of flakes. All sound was muffled.

'It's a long, long time since I was out in the snow. Long since I saw it. I suppose the land and hills are like ghosts now.'

He held out a hand and closed the fist and rubbed the fingers together on the flakes he had trapped.

'Your mother could tell you, son, if she were alive, about the frost and the snow of seventeenforty. If the wind blows, it'll smother your house and Knockanee.'

'God shield us,' said the son. 'Come in or you'll freeze to death. The whole parish will think you're daft, standing there with the snow in your hand.'

VIII

The wind held off until the heavens were free and the thaw had broken the snow into ugly rugged patches that oozed water. The stream filled up, swishing down the rocks to the swollen yellow river that soused the lowland fields. That was by Christmas Eve when Mr. Dundee's tenants, a man from every house, walked down in their Sunday clothes to Lacken House, to the barn in the yard, where, by a custom the master had made, they were given every one of them a few pounds of beef or mutton cut from beasts slaughtered specially for the purpose. Pleading, winking, arguing in undertones lest the master in the house should hear, they begged for extra bits and scraps from the stable-boy who hacked off shares with fine lordly strokes. By way of thanks, the tenants waited till the doling out was completed and then they gathered before the front portico of the house to lift their hats and the gobs of meat in their hands and to give cheers for Mr. Dundee. This they almost forgot to do in the flurry that strange news caused.

'There was a man in the yard,' said Donnacha the son, telling the story to his father, 'and he had come up from the sea in the morning with a message for Mr. Dundee. He wasn't too steady on his feet or too lively with his tongue. The master has a generous hand with the bottle for strangers at Christmas time. The stranger said that three fishermen had been driven out one night and they had seen a mighty long awful line of vessels passing by in the early morning. They were the French, coming to take Ireland.

'The stranger says that he spoke himself with the fishermen. He swears it. He says there were scores of ships, filling the sea to the sky, all going westward in the bad weather. He says the people were wild, some with fear and some with joy. Soldiers rode in and the people kept indoors, not even daring to peep out, and the gentry are forming bands to guard the coast. They'll be after the United men now, I tell you.

'But,' concluded the son in scorn, 'I believe he's a brazen liar. I heard him telling different stories entirely to other men and once he said that what he knew had been told him by...'

'A woman told me that a woman told her that another woman told her! Geese-gabble!' snapped Donnacha Ruadh.

Yet his mockery had no edge in it. A fervour was squeezing the blood from his heart. His son's story, for all its jibings and disbelief, had breathed on old desires, and in the weak rekindled flame of them a vision fashioned itself, wavered smokily, hung clear and sharp for one instant and subsided to the ashes. News like that had been in the air many times during his life, indeed as early as he could remember. How easily was hope raised! He was young, barefoot, eager for learning in the world and in books in his birthplace in Clare where the Shannon spread wide and serene out towards the thundering sea, and the old men of that time, gossiping by the turf-fires of nights about the battle for Limerick's walls, always regretted that the hosting of ships from France had come too late with succour for the defeated. The older men were dead and he was in his prime, married, schoolmastering, full of himself, and again they were talking of the French and of the Prince of the Stuarts who nearly had the lost Three Crowns in his grasp. Men made songs even about the help that would come some day and about the sea-pounded fleets and the flags. Fools they were – and he had been one of them – cracked, story-making fools, too weak and too fearful to do themselves what they wished others to do for them, too packed with pride to take and cherish the little peace and the little comfort there was to be had of the world. Now, here they were chattering again, all their loose tongues set wagging by the gossip of a befuddled stranger. But, if it were true about the ships, what then? Desires kindled again and his slow blood throbbed. All he had seen of the traffic of the seas off the Clare coast, in the northern German town when he was returning home a spoiled priest, in Waterford where the masts were as thick as trees in a wood, and in the Land of the Fish, all now mingled and in a flash became definite anew: a long line of vessels rising up with the wind from the edge of the sky, their hulls dark and their bellying crowded sails pallid in the thin sea-shine of the early morning, and foam streaming back from prows set for the coast of Ireland.

'Sit down,' said the son. 'Sit down, I tell you. The house is not big enough for hobbling around it like that.'

'Why do you be exciting him with such stories?' the housewife complained.

'They'll tear through the towns after the red-coats and they'll drive them before them out of the country. They'll put the run on them, son. They'll... we'll have the land.'

'Father, father,' said Eibhlín, going to him and holding his arm, 'stop it, stop this talk.'

'The stranger,' the son declared deliberately, 'was a liar.'

'A liar, son. Aye, I was forgetting,' said he sitting down. 'A liar, a tale-bearer making his own tales for Christmas drink.'

They ate their Christmas dinner, picked the rare bones clean, drank their soup to the last drop, and thanked God they had so much and that the time was peaceful.

On St. Stephen's Day Mr. Dundee left his houseful of company and rode around from tenant to tenant, saying briefly that although he was not quite sure of the truth of the rumours, it would be best for every one of them to behave cautiously and to speak of nothing, even among themselves, that could be taken as disloyalty to the Government. He was smiling, amiable, and red-faced from riding in the north-wind and from drinking at Lacken.

On the morrow the people of Knockanee were at their doors, looking down at the small figures on the valley road. A straggling line of soldiers, their red coats and white breeches splashed and soaking, rode by sullenly. They dragged a gun with them that must have toppled into a ditch for it was caked thick with dark mud and its cover flapped. At the three houses at the cross-roads they halted, swarming about the place and demanding drink, food and fodder till, it was rumoured a woman was frightened out of her wits and fell into a fit from which she recovered terrified and talking senselessly. Their officer, it was said, who was little heeded by his men, took a boy and jammed him against a wall and shouted about the French and the United men and spies. No one could decide whether this was only gossip, but it was true, as everybody in Knockanee swore, that hot, hasty words had passed between the officer and Mr. Dundee in the yard of Lacken. People who had been visiting in farther places came home with all kinds of queer stories about a village being burned beside the sea by the soldiers, about ships, about yeomen armed to the teeth meeting in the big houses, and about men being dragged off to gaol in Waterford and Clonmel.

The old year blew itself out in a screaming, cleaving gale that laid trees low, lifted thatched roofs on the lee-side of the valley, tumbled ricks in yards, and finally dwindled away southward towards the sea. The skies were cloudless then, and with the change a lazy south wind brought the first faint warmth of the coming spring. Only on the mountains, almost one in their paleness with the bleached sky, was there any of the snow.

X

'Will you go, Eibhlín, to the door,' said Donnacha Ruadh, 'and see where is that crying coming from? I hear it. Listen. There it is from the other end of Knockanee.'

The man of the house had gone down to speak and bargain with Mr. Dundee about the rent that had fallen due. Eibhlín and the old man were sitting before the fire which, in heating the house that had its door closed, made the air heavy and sleep-giving. The odours of baking griddle bread and roasted potatoes mixed with the acrid blue smoke from a damp log that spluttered in a red bed of embers.

Eibhlín yawned, pushing back grey wisps of hair from her face. 'I was in a doze,' said she, laughing sadly.

'Hurry woman. Listen.'

She opened the door, shivering as the chill evening enveloped her, and gazed down the fall of the hill with eyes narrowed against the sunset. She sniffed, coughed, and then ran out.

'Come here,' she called. 'Come here. There are houses afire. Four of them, Mother of God! The smoke is in clouds.'

At the threshold, Donnacha Ruadh said, 'Help me, woman. What is it? Are you dumb?'

They heard the crying clearly then and in the midst of it, more definite than the hoarse bawling of men, the wailing of a young child.

'It's down on us, woman.'

They both coughed as the smoke, driven from below them by the southerly breeze and clinging to the fields, floated past. It was smut-laden, thick, bitter with the reek of the rotting straw and the stale furze of the thatching.

'Eibhlín, for God's sake, speak.'

'There are men with red coats. They're running around. The cattle are all galloping across the ditches and walls. There isn't a man of Knockanee in sight. Only the women, screeching and dragging things from the houses. There are red flames all over the place. Stop, Tomás,' she cried. 'Tomás, boy, what is it?'

A boy, racing up alongside the stream, stopped at a gap in a wall, and with his hands on the stones he shrilled across his shoulder, 'Get out of your house. They're after the men. Get out. They struck Mr. Dundee and he's all blood.' He rattled the stones from the wall as he leaped and ran.

'Here,' said Eibhlín, 'stand there. I'll get what I can. They're moving this way.'

'They're mad. They're staring mad.'

She left him standing and coughing in the swirling eddying smoke that lifted and broke against the hillside.

Her face white and her mouth set, she trotted back into the house. With darting hands she spread blankets on the floor, and piled clothes into them, dishes, a cake of bread; and making a bundle, she carried it out and laid it beside her father-in-law. Back again to fill a sack with the geegaws of the house: a headless china coloured statue, two battered brass candlesticks, a little copper pan, balls of wool and thread, a few knives and pewter spoons, a wooden ladle, and lastly good shoes and boots. Into the bodice of her dress she thrust a crucifix that had been carved crudely but strongly with a knife thirty years before against her wedding day by a man of her own country. She paused, swinging her gaze around anxiously and grasping at the air with her lined, loose-skinned hands that had patiently put together, treasured, washed and scrubbed the small things of her house, and then blocking her open mouth with her fist, she shuddered from head to foot and moaned. Her pain passed. It was numbed by her desire to save what she could. Hauling the sack to her shoulders, she stamped out under the weight to the stooped, wheezing man who faced into the choking smoke. She passed by him and stumbled up the slope to a ring of black-thorns that were rooted in the clenching rocks above, beside the stream. Below, the screaming of the child had come to an end. Men alone spoke, shortly, too busy for many words.

Donnacha Ruadh went forward, downward, gathering up strength feverishly. He felt the heat in the smoke now and a spark stung his cheek like a wasp. Then, not knowing he was almost invisible, he stopped, deliberately filled his lungs with the charred air, and in sideslipping shrieks he harangued: 'May God wither up your souls. You're not soldiers. House burners. Murderers. May the French spit ye and spike ye. You're not men.'

'You'll ruin us.' It was a woman, running by, who spoke.

'Scarecrow! Ragman!' he heard, in English.

'Is there no man in Knockanee?' he tried to say, spluttering on the smoke.

Eibhlín was beside him, dragging on his arm, panting. He went with her. The blackthorns were more than two hundred paces away and every twenty or thirty paces she halted to release great gulps of air from her bursting chest. When they reached the thorns, he fell on his face and she left him lie.

There were other women down behind the rocks, the children sitting together, peering out between the twisted boles of the trees. They did not turn their unwinking look from the waving flags of flame that grew fiercely red in the half-light and the gathering darkness when other women, other children and old men crept in from the fields.

'Ah!' said Eibhlín, and gave a long-drawn sigh, 'they're doing it now.'

The day thinned out altogether and everything was in shadow except the hill, and yet they did not move but took the wineglow of the dying and rising fires on their petrified, grey and unprotesting faces.

XI

In a broken procession with their returned menfolk, they came down the paths and cart tracks to Lacken House where, like straws and leaves and dead twigs cast in a ruck into a corner, they gathered in the yard.

The barn was opened. They trooped in, finding places to sit or to stretch in exhaustion among the sacks, the straw and the heaped potatoes. A yellow glow presently seeped down from two oil-lamps hung on the wall, and even with this kind light the people did not look long on one another lest they should discover pain like crawling worms in the lit eyes. An infant lately born whimpered.

Dundee stood in the doorway, his arms outstretched to the jambs. On his head he wore a bandage and down the front of his riding coat there was a long rent. He smiled faintly, nodding at the clustered heads before him.

'Yes,' he said, deep in his chest, in English. 'You'll not suffer. Why did it happen? I don't know. You did no wrong.' Bursting into a vibrant shouting, he added, 'It's a pity, by the Lord God, the wind prevented the French from...' He checked himself, and dropped his voice again. 'They burned Knockanee because, they said, the members of a traitorous society had been in the place. They spoke of some man from the north who had escaped from Clonmel. I knew it was false. You would have told me, wouldn't you?'

Heads bobbed all together in assent.

'The wind is a strange beast,' he continued, drawing his hand down his broad red face, and blinking. 'The elements are as fickle... What am I talking about?' He blew out his breath and wiped his face again with his hand. Beads of sweat glistened on his forehead. 'Here,' he added, 'I want someone to build a fire in the yard. There are potatoes there. There'll be meat from the kitchen for the women and children. We'll build the houses again, never you fear. If anyone is injured or hurt...' He laughed then, saying, 'Where's that old man? The man who dared His Majesty's army? The man who shouted. He's my man. He is.' Weakness sapped at him again and gesturing he ambled away across the yard, feeling before him with his toes as if he were walking on an ice-bound pool. But he had lifted the terror from the people ,and they began to talk and to discover one another loudly like exiles come home from far and friendless countries.

'Where's my son?' Donnacha Ruadh whispered. He was cold with a weariness that soaked through him like winter-water. A child was sprawling beside him, its fingers dug into his coat, and he rubbed its head.

Eibhlín answered. 'He's here.'

'Yes, I'm here, father.'

'Your house is gone, son.'

'The walls stand. Couldn't it be worse?'

'Come to me. Look.' He rummaged inside his shirt and dragged out the leather bag. 'That's for you, for yourself and herself. Sovereigns, five of them. You'll have a fine roof with that, and no debts. Oh! God, give me sleep.' He lay back against a barrel. The woman held his arm as she had held it since they cowered among the thorns and since they began the trudge from the smoke-tormented hillside and the broken houses. From where she sat she could see broad bands of steady brilliant light falling across the yard and against walls and gables from all the windows of Lacken House. Men were moving and throwing dancing shadows and already, so soon, there was quiet laughter. She, too, leaned back and closed her eyes.

PART TWO

Flame

Howl, howl, howl, howl! O, you are men of stones:
Had I your tongues and eyes, I'd use them so
That heaven's vault should crack.

(King Lear.)

I pity the fools who always live in strife
While near them, every day, the graves are fed;
No sooner have the aged wheezed out weak life
But biers come bearing young and strong men, dead.

(From the Irish.)

'If we have received good things at the hand of God,
why should we not receive evil?'

(JOB ii. 10.)

CHAPTER IV

The fan of the winds

I

If that wintertide had been cruel there would have been, they were sure, many a young child and an ailing woman and an old man dead of the hardship in Knockanee. The mild breath of the wind that had thawed the snow and thereby swelled Lacken river to a yellow, foam-curled flood, did not depart but stayed and became even kindlier. Only in the night during the frosts, in the barn with its stone cold floor beneath the straw and the barrels and the potatoes, was it difficult to keep your limbs or your exposed face from being numbed. The cold rolled through your blood. The men occasionally stood up in the darkness to stamp their bare feet on the straw, now flattened to the floor. Children whimpered, hardly knowing what troubled them, till the women chafed, and petted them with a 'There now, you'll be as right as rain. There now, child.'

Donnacha Ruadh often felt the cold in his bones in which the marrow seemed to be ice. Sleep at best was thin, buzzing with voices and the innumerable movements of the dark. Pains burrowed in his joints like hard bristly burrs. When, in the morning, he sensed the pale sunlight from the open door, he would yawn and his shoulders would, by the effort, become stiff and strained. Eibhlín fed him, mostly with potato mash, sometimes with hot porridge, and once with a piece of buttered bread that the housekeeper had sent out for the children. All the time he walked, lay down, submitted to the pushing and jostling, ate and drank as if nothing were happening or could happen to him at all.

'A great brave old man he is, worth the whole lot of us,' he heard someone say; and that was worth waiting for.

The men, with Mr. Dundee to direct them, went up to Knockanee to examine the blackened walls, the clods of thatch that still smouldered or were warm to the hands, the charred tables and chairs, and the ashes, grey and black and everywhere deep on the clay floors. Dundee rode, his low-crowned hat set on his bandaged head. Anyone, he offered, who did not wish to return and rebuild his house could go if he pleased from

Knockanee; but not one departed.

The burning had been done hastily. Small hay and straw ricks had been left untouched, while roofs of old straw and furze, soaked by snow and rain, had caught fire and lost it again. The slated house had escaped free, except its door which was smashed into bits. All could have been worse.

Working fast, they set about raising the houses once more. Every cart from Lacken House and the few carts in Knockanee in which the people had a share, were used for drawing the pasty clay for the broken walls and the timber from the grove on the river bank. The clay was puddled, beaten and mixed with straw, and slapped down to top the walls which were finally coped with flat stones. Down in the grove where leave had been given to fell marked trees, the work was short and hard. Floodwater from the river was ankle-deep and bitter cold there, the cart-wheels slid unturning in the mud, and one man, although he had been warned by shouts, was struck by a bough of a crashing tree and had to be taken, with a broken arm, on horseback to the doctor in Ballybreen. Men who never had a fair rooftree much less a roof that did not let in the weather, now had sound roofs of straw, hay and good timber. There would be, too, fine fires on the hearthstones.

'The soldiers did us a good turn,' one man remarked in half-earnest, and he was told to keep his tongue still, for stories were being told about how the soldiers, yet on the move, had put terror in far townlands, burning a house here and there, tying men to trees or to carts for a flogging before the people; and it was told that, over in the streets of Clonmel, they had torn a green dress from a gentlewoman and all her clothes along with it and sent her stark-naked and screaming through the town. Whenever Dundee was questioned for the truth of the rumours, he always said, 'We've had enough trouble for a lifetime. But it's not finished.'

One by one the families left the barn for their homes. Donnacha Ruadh was among the last to leave because his son's house was among the last to be repaired, it being so far up the hillside towards the pass. They carried him back in a cart, with Eibhlín, three neighbour's children, and a small sack of bread and apples that Mr. Dundee had given him a present, saying, 'That's for an old man who wasn't afraid.'

'Afraid? But I was, sir. I was only foolish, out of my mind. I couldn't see what was happening.' But all the way up the hillside he was repeating, 'Did you catch what he said to me? I'm not bragging, but I did dare them didn't I, Eibhlín?'

With the fire lighting and his feet, bootless, towards the heat, the cold thawed at last in his bones. After Eibhlín had washed him, his first washing for weeks, and combed his beard and fed him with hot milk and fresh griddle bread, he began to bask like a cat in the comfort.

'If there wasn't the burnt smell,' said he, 'to remind us, it would be like coming to a new house, Eibhlín.'

'It would. I wish I had my sons with me, or one of them anyway. It's not easy to have an empty house and we going grey.'

'They'll come back. Hish, woman, they'll come back.'

I I

When you are blind, with the power of sight turned inward to things once seen and not forgotten, and with the hearing keyed up tightly to respond to every breath, and when at the same time you are old, so used by all the big and petty blundering of men that nothing can happen again to weigh down or exalt your heart, you can sit on the threshold of two worlds and you can judge and see better than the men with the life in their eyes and the discontent in their blood.

When they say on a spring morning that it's a fine bright day, God bless it, you can discern the squeezed-out notes of a thrush, rising clear above the swallow-chittering in an outhouse and the hasty hungry chirping of sparrows foraging among the chickens; and you can see in your mind where you have stored up summer, the best morning of all mornings: level sunlight on slopes and lowland lawny meadows that cast off faint mist and are fresh and lush for cattle; pools dark and still, or ripple-webbed by early rising insects; pools capturing the full light and holding in themselves the heavy trees and sentinel rushes upside down; and running water enlacing rocks on which the dark green moss is already becoming caked and dry; smoke, above the houses, coiling up from stirred embers; drowsy eyes and the hunger after sleep. Or at twilight, when talk is at its best, the neighbours gather around the house, on the walls or on the grass, every man saying as he comes to the gathering that it is a great evening, you can almost feel the grey light on your hands and you can hear quietness being drawn gently across the land, across the slopes and the pools where insects hum in deep damp shadows, across the bird-shielding bushes and the dun fading houses from which lamps and rushlights and candles shine dim. You sit between two worlds, knowing your daily dismemberment, your body's sundering, your heart's weakening, and you do not wonder why these things happen. The day goes and men die. So it was with Donnacha Ruadh.

On the warm days Eibhlín brought him out of the house in which her own loneliness was like a secretly blowing chill draught, and left him by a wall where he sat or whence he made his way for talk, guided by the sound of men digging in the stony fields. The men were working again as if there had been no such winter as they had known and no burning. He heard them at their old arguments about potato-seed, straying sheep and the right of way on struggling paths, and it gave him joy. The hardness in them, the rock in them that made them endure, was unbroken.

Seeing his years stretching behind him like a toothed line of mountains, he was sure this hardness was everlasting, for it had never yielded. True it was they had lost the common lands to the lords, and that they had died, frozen like boards, in a famine. They begged on the roads, whined, and then cursed when the pursy men were out of hearing; and for a few months' rent, they clutched and grasped until meanness was bred in their souls. They stood in the ditch out of the way when the carriages of the gentry went by, and they touched their hats, bowed, almost going on their bellies like hounds, to the commanding voices that could take all or leave all. They should have withered away. Yet, they were there, when all the waters and storms had passed, clinging like sea-creatures to the rocks, as he himself clung to life.

'We'll never be finished, son,' he said. 'I say it. We will not. Ever.'

His son, spade in hand in the field, looked up, wiped the sweat up into his thick hairs, and shook his head sorrowfully. There's no knowing, he thought, what kind of notions the old will take, what it is that goes on in their minds and drives sudden lonely words to their lips.

III

The neighbours tried not to treat him as a childish irritable old man when they dropped in of nights, and once more he was called, as he had not been called for many years, by the name of 'Master.' 'Master,' one of them or the son himself, would ask, 'what do you say to that?' whenever talk ended in a wrangle about the French and their wars, the wages going for hired

70

work over in Cork or up in Tipperary, or what the priest had really meant in a sermon. Awaiting his answer patiently they would lean from their stools and watch him curiously, noting the tiny pats he gave his knees, the nods, the sluggish struggling with the cracked voice, and the vacant eyes.

'Well, men, when I was on the Continent – I was a lad then and I had seen more of the world than all of you'll ever see – when I was in Italy I saw the country where there's a war. It was flat as the floor and brown, and the heat, the heat, men, you could feel it pricking the back of your neck and raising blisters on you. There was a town, all big white houses and mansions, and dogs crawling around in the dust, and everybody asleep for the evening. I was on my last legs. And a young one came to me and brought me to a door and gave me wine. It's wine they drink, rich and poor, like water, men. Aye, it was a cool house she brought me to, and she was... Ah! what am I talking about? Go on, men, with your own argument and don't be heeding me.'

'How long ago was that, master?'

'How long? How long since what?'

'Since you drank wine in a house in Italy?'

'How long?' The fingers plucked at the breeches, and the eyes were almost wrinkled shut with a sly smile. 'It must be twenty years.'

'Father, what's that?'

'Wait now, wait.' The head was shaken vigorously. 'I was thinking of other things. It must be more than sixty years. Aye, sixty years, men.'

One night a man inquired if he ever made verses now, and this man went on to recite pieces of the long rambling poem about the journey to the Land of the Fish, the adventures at sea and the fight, and as the lines were rolled off, the company eagerly helped by joining in. Vainly the old man attempted to interrupt for corrections but they ignored his outstretched hands and his pleading. They blundered through the poem as best they could, slipping in lines of their own and nonsense and uproar, skipping, laughing, till they had Donnacha Ruadh sitting bewildered, with tears creeping wearily down the tangled lines of his face. And he said:

'You don't forget me, men. You do not. God bless you.

'Over in Slieve Gua, in the true mountains where I was school-mastering once, they could sing you my songs. But you, too, don't forget me.

'Aye, I made a poem. It's for Tadhg Gaolach O Suilleabhain

whose hymns you sing now and again below in the chapel.'

'Faith, then,' a neighbour cut in, sniggering, 'I know a few stories about the same Tadhg.'

'Well, damn your soul, keep your stories if that's all you know about him. That's all you have about the dead: stories of the deeds you'd like to be doing if you had the courage. Keep them. You'll get no poem from me now. Anyway it's in the Latin and... keep your stories, you boors.'

And then his audience would be a company of silent men, sitting around by the walls, their heads down, their ears waiting for the end of the blurted spluttering rage. The rage and the jabbing stick, not the words that they could barely catch, would silence them, but he himself would set them at ease once more: 'Ah! don't mind me, men. Forgive me. Why don't you put a check on me?'

When they would leave and go to their beds and when the cool night air, fresh and wind-stirred, would bring life back to the dead breath of the house, he would brighten up and beg to be left sitting a little longer beside the fire for a few more companionable words before he lay down in the dark.

'Why do they come, son? It was not always like this.'

'Not since the children went! – Go on with you. Looking for praise you are!'

'I'm glad of it anyway,' said Eibhlín.

'I'm glad of it myself, daughter. Company in the house is a second hearth. Now, why were you crying to yourself the other night, woman? It won't help you.' He tried to stop his words but they were out, and he heard the sudden indrawing of her breath and the long, barely controlled sigh. He scraped the floor with his feet and pretended to search for the stick although he could feel its weight resting on his thigh.

IV

One great loss there was out of the burning of Knockanee. The man who had been struck by the falling tree, died. During the weeks after his return from the doctor, he had not complained of the broken arm at all or of anything; yet the flesh thinned on him till his sunken eyes looked darkly out of his skull; and his wife said that sometimes, when he thought she wasn't nearby, she noticed how he spread his hands on his chest and stomach and gripped and groaned for breath. 'I knew,' said she, 'what he was afraid of. I knew why he wouldn't complain. He was afraid of yielding. He was afraid he couldn't work and pay rent. He was afraid he'd lose the home and the bit of land and see myself and the children on the roads begging.' After she had cried herself sick amongst the women, she was herself again at the wake: dry-eyed, gaunt, and terribly calm.

They brought Donnacha Ruadh to the wake. Eibhlín led him in from the little yard where men stood close together in groups to speak low of the dead and of death in the palely lit summery darkness; in through the pipe-reeking kitchen where the people sat with the fatherless children; down to the second room of the house in which two candles burned oilily and the women crouched with the housewife whose still unmoving face was shadowed in the hood of her shawl.

Donnacha Ruadh tried to kneel and then shook his head at the failure of his effort. 'It's I who should be lying under the sheets,' said he in a whisper. He bowed, leaning on his stick, his hat between his fingers, his shoulders swaying gently and regularly to the rhythm of some prayer he uttered. Haltingly, he spoke aloud so that the stooped womenfolk lifted their red smouldering eyes: 'A poem about the dead man should be made and about his brave strong heart. I'm not the man to make it, for my time's done. But whatever would be said by the greatest poet of the land couldn't surpass the praise his own woman gave him, and she full of her loss. God rest him and keep you and your kin, woman.'

They guided him back to the kitchen and made way for him on a short stool before the fire where, for a little while, he remained still. He refused the filled, kindled pipe that was put in his hands. Whiskey from the jar that Mr. Dundee had sent was passed round in cups and mugs.

'It'll go to your head, father,' Eibhlín warned him. 'You shouldn't drink it.'

Saying that he was never a man to break a custom for the sake of a weak head, he drank down the whiskey hastily. It quickened his slow blood, and soon, although the room and the people seemed to withdraw from him, he began to be restless with the desire of telling them something, he knew not what exactly, that needed telling as sorely as a heart-wounding secret. He wagged his head, searching for the thing that escaped him, and jerked back and forth on the stool and changed the grip of his hands on his stick. The padding and thudding of feet, booted and bare, continued across the floor as neighbours came in from the night, went to the second room, prayed and returned to the packed kitchen where the forgotten fire was grey ash, or to the gossiping groups in the yard, the boys and the girls watching for the chance of slipping away unnoticed in couples. Once a dog that came sniffing in by the doorposts was sent out again yelping from the jab of a boot and the people said 'Hush, hush'; and once, outside beyond the yard-wall, a girl laughed out loud and stopped of a sudden as if she remembered how near to her was dust from which the soul had gone. Then, Donnacha Ruadh found himself talking.

He found himself talking, not about the living and the dead, but of the passing of the poets and of the petty rhymers left in their stead. He thought – but the words were really lost in the flickering and guttering of his voice – that he was saying clearly: 'Isn't it a woeful night for us when there's no poet living fit to mourn in verse the man whose house was burned in a great burning and who died at the building? I knew the poets. You, you have only the stories. I knew Aindrias Mac Craith the rogue, and Liam Inglis the friar, and Sean O Tuama with his tavern; and I knew Piaras Mac Gearailt who had high blood in his veins; and Piaras lost his land and saved a patch by turning heretic...' He winced. If Piaras had swopped a religion for a religion, had not he himself done likewise? Had he not tried to be a heretic with a heart that would not be still? The twinge that passed through his soul like the stab of an aching tooth left him hot for a second, and he lifted his voice to quell an old lurking memory. 'And I knew Tadhg; Tadhg who was my friend, and he's gone after the rest. And I, Donnacha Ruadh Mac Conmara, an old bag of dry feeble bones, await my turn. There's nothing remaining, nothing of the lords who fought in terrible battles and reaped defeat, nor of their lands and their mansions: only ourselves, sitting down like this in a small house to lament the dead.'

He came to himself to find Eibhlín pulling at his shoulders and shaking him and hushing, and the kitchen as quiet as the lower room in which the dead man lay.

'What was he saying at all?'

'I could only catch a word or two.'

'God help him.'

'Master, you'll outlive us all.'

'True, we'll all be gone and you'll be alive.'

'But tell me, what was it he was mourning?'

'I'd say all the generations that ever were.'

'He seemed to be talking with them.'

'Hush! don't let him hear. The blind see more than we see with our living eyes.'

74

'Father,' Eibhlín murmured patiently in his ear. 'Father, come on home. It's time, father. It's a long walk. Say no more. They know...'

He pushed her away and leaned against the wall, his head sunken. His tongue was dry and leathery in his mouth. Behind his forehead, as in a blaze of light from a noonday summer sun, a muttering and debating of many strange and incomprehensible voices began, and although he tried to listen he could not lay hold on anything except on a music that went with the voices, contrasting with their deep base notes; and the music, he recognised, was a slow, anguished, measured keen for mighty dead and lords and men of kingly blood; and to the inner chorus he heard another voice added, his own, speaking in a monotone: Out of the depths I have cried to thee, O Lord: Lord, hear my voice. Let thine ears be attentive to the voice of my supplication... From the morning watch even unto night, let Israel hope in the Lord. From the morning watch...; and so it continued, endless, humming, muttering, rising and falling like a wind against a great house. Through it all, he heard but did not heed the modulated babble around him in the kitchen; men talking about their farms, their dead kindred, accidents, the French, the soldiers, the seller of spectacles who escaped from Clonmel, Mr. Dundee; and all their talk seemed to belong to another world, to a dream that was dissolving as he sank deeper and deeper into the solemnly chanting imperturbable company of the dead.

He started up against the wall and bumped his head. The shock brought him to himself and he put his hands before him foolishly. His son was commanding sharply, 'Come on, now. You're falling asleep. Get up. We'll drive you home in a cart.' He submitted in a daze, trying to recall what remote land his soul had visited, what music had blown about his ears, what mighty grief had risen in a tide for his drowning.

V

Near the time of the hay-mowing a young man came over the pass of Knockanee from the north, one day not long after the dawn. It was Donnacha, the son, out driving sheep, who first sighted him as he struggled up the sheep-path, slipping on the loose rain-scoured stones and stooped against the climb. Donnacha sat down to watch and wait.

The young man laboured up, halting with head down at every

75

dozen steps and not lifting his eyes to the sky at all. Below him and behind him was the slope down to the narrow valley that was brightened only by placid, shining bog-pools and clumps of yellow furze in bloom. In a declivity in the sheep-track where small stones like eggs had been cluttered together by some torrent, he tripped, and with his arms waving, toppled sideways to the thin sod. Donnacha, alarmed, rose to his feet, but the stranger was up again and climbing to the saddle of the pass and his breath was whooing from his chest. When they were within ten paces of each other, Donnacha said: 'That's hard work for the early morning, young fellow.'

The young man came to a standstill, his body erect but sideways, one foot turned behind him as though he were preparing for a downward run. He was without pack or bundle or stick, and his two arms, empty-handed, were tensed and crooked at his sides. The left armpit of the long frieze coat he wore was burst; rags of a shirt covered his broad heaving chest; the knees of his breeches, muddy and clinging to his thighs, were unloosed; and the left one of his bare beslimed feet was wrapped in a piece of cloth, one end of which trailed among the stones. His face, by contrast with his jet-black cropped hair and the streak of stubble on his jaws and the eyes glittering black and restless in the early sun, was as hard and white as marble. Slanting from the right eyesocket, down across the nose and cheeks to the left jaw-point, was a thin even smudge, like a line of grime or soot. He advanced a few steps, stopped, bent of a sudden, staggering with the effort, snatched up a stone and approached with his arm raised for casting.

Unmoving, Donnacha drawled, 'Welcome to you! I don't think you'll find much need for that stone in Knockanee.'

The black eyes blinked and the mouth opened. There was a sigh.

'Don't be afraid, man,' Donnacha added leisurely. 'We're not bad people or King's men.' And he moved as he asked, 'Your face, what gave you that welt? Great God!'

The stone dropped to the heather. Donnacha caught him around the shoulders and felt the squirm of the muscles beneath his hands. A wry smile eased the tight mouth that opened and slowed only toothless gums, swollen behind thick lips.

'It's fighting you were. There's my house, man. Come with me and not a soul will lift a hand against you.'

'It's turning warm,' said the man, slowly and huskily.

'You'll sleep,' Donnacha murmured.

His father was sitting inside the doorway where the sunshine beamed and almost killed the fire.

'Father, get up. We have a visitor. Give him that chair. Where's Eibhlín? There, sit now.'

'Down with one of the neighbours, I suppose.'

'I'll find her. You're as safe as the priest now, friend. Rest easy there.'

The son went out, calling his wife's name.

Donnacha Ruadh, standing by the wall, listened. The man was breathing quicker, groaning faintly with every breath. Suddenly the groaning ceased, there was a whimper, the chair rattled against the wall, and Donnacha Ruadh knew that the man had slipped to the floor. Eibhlín was running in and her husband behind her.

'Is it the hunger?' asked Donnacha Ruadh.

The couple lifted the man to the low bed in the corner and while the husband tried to spoon whiskey between the bruised lips, the housewife bathed the forehead with a wet cloth.

'Tell me,' Donnacha Ruadh asked again, 'is it the hunger in some place once more?'

'Hold him up,' said Eibhlín. 'His clothes are soaking. I'll take them off.' She removed the coat.

Then, like a man uttering blasphemy coldly, the husband spoke: 'Go get warm water. And a knife.'

She cried out, 'God it's raw!'

'The blood's dry. I'll cut the shirt. Hurry, woman.'

'Is it the hunger?'

Donnacha the son whispered: 'He was lashed.'

It was the woman who was self-controlled now, until her task with the man was done. 'Put him on his face,' she said. 'Get me the unsalted butter and a strip of cloth from the press. Keep away. This is my work.'

The father and the son stood silent, all their minds dark.

Before the woman had finished, he came to himself and asked for water of which she let him drink a few mouthfuls only. Naked he lay face-downwards and she lifted the bed-clothes gently about his shoulders. He burrowed his face into the pillow and soon they heard him sobbing quietly into rest. Before she could give him the warm milk with bread crumbled into it, he was dead asleep.

'Whist, woman,' said Donnacha the son. 'Cease your crying.'

'It might have been one of my own.'

'Go and see if you can find a piece of meat. He'll need the nourishment. Where's my father?'

'He's outside, can't you hear him talking to himself?'

Out in the sun, alone, Donnacha Ruadh was saying, 'God, why

don't you strike or give us a sign? What have we done? What have we done?

'Ah! there's no peace.'

At sunset the stranger awoke and sitting up painfully, he looked around him at the rushlight, the coats hanging on the wall, the hearth with its simmering pot, the dresser with its few white plates and mugs, the ropes and leather on the stool beneath the little unglazed window in which twilight dimmed reluctantly. His gaze came to rest on the glowing fire and he smiled. The woman and the men waited.

'So I was sleeping,' he said, blubbing the words from his thick lips. He ran his right forefinger along the welt on his face and added; 'I'll not trouble the house any farther. I'll be going. If you please, woman, give me my clothes.'

'Are you hungry?' Donnacha asked.

The man nodded.

'You'll not go hungry from this house. Here, I'll help you with your clothes; and here's a shirt of mine, if you don't mind wearing it.'

It was not easy to dress him, for every time he lifted his arms, he stretched the dry skin and the muscles of his back. He was quite unable to stoop and to lace the pair of old shoes, a little too large, that Donnacha gave him. When he was dressed, he was restless, his eyes turned towards the closed door, and once, at the sound of a hen fluttering in the thatch, he started to his feet. They made him sit still until he had eaten bread and drunk soup.

'You're a Tipperary man,' Donnacha Ruadh remarked. 'I know by your accent. Tipperary men are good men.'

'No questions,' said the son.

'Oh!' the man replied, laughing dryly, 'I've no fear of you.'

'You needn't say a word if you don't wish,' Donnacha Ruadh muttered. 'We know. The world's going mad with burning and heating and killing people who only want to be left alone.'

'They burned Knockanee.'

'I heard of that,' the stranger said. 'And you can have my story to put with it,' he added bitterly. 'You can have my story to put with it if ever you get your hands upon them that do the destruction. I'll remember yours. By the Lord God of Heaven, someday...'

He put the soup-bowl by with shaking hands and then sat upright, with his elbows close to his sides to ease any strain on his back.

78

'It's true, I'm a Tipperary man.'

'Ah! the old head,' said Donnacha Ruadh, 'can recognise an accent yet.'

'Hush!' the son warned.

'Last fair-day I went to Clogheen. You know Clogheen at the foot of the mountains, away beyond there. A good journey! Judkin Fitzgerald the Sheriff was there, and men with him, armed and drunk. Aye, Judkin Fitzgerald whose name we won't forget. Now, I never had a hand in any deed against the law. Never was I a party to any United men or whoever they are. I live outside Clogheen with my brothers and my sister.'

The stranger paused and clasped his hands together on his knees. He seemed to be forgetting where he was and what he was telling when, softly, the old man said, 'And you'll live there again, please God, my friend.'

In a lower tone, the teller continued: 'I was after selling a heifer and I was walking the street at noon, as any man will on a fair, when Judkin Fitzgerald rode in, with his eyes rolling in his red face. The people of the town scattered like flies before your hand. Into the houses and shops and taverns they ran. I took cover, too, in a house that had the door unlatched. The people of the house were looking through the window and not letting themselves be seen. Out on the street a crowd of people were caught between two bands of the Sheriff's men and there wasn't one of them that raised his voice then.

'Over beside a shop there was a cart and it unyoked and heeled up, I saw Fitzgerald's men dragging a poor man, a neighbour of our own, and pitching him down on his knees and tying him with halters to the wheel. His face bled. It was knocked against the hub. Then they cut his coat from his back with a knife. Nobody at all was saying anything except Fitzgerald. He was shouting at the top of his voice about what he'd do to United men and traitors and to the women of the place. You'd think that the man tied was dead. You'd think that until Fitzgerald got down from his horse and staggered. The man was screaming then.

'Fitzgerald had a whip, a leather thing like a switch, and when he cut the air with it, I could hear the swish of it in the house where I was. His men were standing quiet when the lashing began, and the man tied was pulling at the halters and lifting his bare back and rocking the cart. I suppose Fitzgerald's men would have said something or cheered if any other man had the whip, but they couldn't that day. Fitzgerald, he was taking delight in it. He was. I think the man fell in a weakness in the halters and it was God's mercy. But Fitzgerald didn't stop.

'In the room where I was a woman began saying, "Stop him! Stop him!" until she was raising her voice to burst your ears. Someone brought her out to the back where she couldn't be heard.

'I don't know what I did when I saw Fitzgerald going on and getting hotter and hotter. But I was out on the street and staggering back from a cut of the whip. The next minute they were all on top of me and the man was taken from the wheel while they were trying to hold me, and I was put in his place. But they didn't put me in his place until they designedly smashed the teeth in the front of my mouth. They did it like this. They held my head. Like this they struck me and Fitzgerald fuming. They put me at the wheel. Then they did it. I don't know how long they were at me.

'I came out of the weakness and I was in an empty room and it was night-time. It took me a long time to get to my feet. I vomited. I thought I was dying, but the blood was only the blood out of my mouth. I held on to the wall and made around to a window that opened on a yard.'

Neither Donnacha nor his wife dared look at the stranger for, noting how he strove to speak evenly, how he controlled himself to tell casually of what had been done to him, they feared that a single glance from them would be a signal for the anger that lay, like swords poised for accurate murderous thrusting, in the pitiless eyes. But Donnacha Ruadh, bewildered by the evil that had been done so freely and hardly knowing whether it was a tale or the truth he had heard, said in the pause: 'It's a queer world. What a day will be the Day of Judgment!'

'I won't wait till then.

'Aye! I was hanging against the window for air when my own name was called from the yard. My brother was calling me and I answered. He told me to be quiet and in a few seconds he was up beside me on a ladder, rubbing my head with his hands as a woman would, and he, a big strong man, bursting his heart. Oh! I'll find them, I'll find them or their breed if I have to wait till your Day of Judgment, old man over there.

'He told me they were around the town and that they flogged another man and stripped a girl and shamed her. I got out through the window but he had to hold me on the ladder for a while because I was weak with the pain of my back. He gave me his coat. And he brought me out across the fields and then I made him go home where he'd be needed. I walked all night into the mountains. Yes, I slept and I ate, out where I don't know. I think I was out of my mind. When I slept a few minutes ago I thought they were holding me again and driving at me and...' It came to an end in a whisper.

'Where are you going?' asked Donnacha Ruadh. 'Why didn't someone help you in Clogheen? Now, if there was...'

'Shut up,' said the son. 'He knows his mind.'

What the stranger's mind was, showed in his face. He was sitting as if his spine and bones were iron and as if he watched, passing before him, all the desire of vengeance fulfilled. Only the old man, now on his feet, muttering to himself in argument, could not see the lips compressed in a snarl and the weal from the whip, hardly more than a faint shading in that tired light of fire and rush, and the unseeing consuming smoulder of the eyes. The woman was shaking her head as she tried not to believe that this was a man, young, whole-hearted, like one of her sons. Her gaze followed him as he arose and walked stiff-legged to the door. He did not turn from the high summer sky where the stars wheeled as she said, 'Stay, if you please. The bed is for you.'

'God be with you,' he answered. 'I'd bring trouble.'

'Follow the path down and you'll meet the road,' the son said.

They listened. The deliberate heavy footsteps dwindled and the last they heard of him was a stone rattling amongst the pebbles of a watercourse; and they could only guess when they heard a dog barking and a cock, startled on the roost, crowing resentfully in a house below near the river, that the man was passing. Donnacha Ruadh was stooped at the doorway to catch the sounds of the night.

'Did you see his face?' Eibhlín asked.

'It was in his voice,' said Donnacha Ruadh, 'and in his step. When all the voices like his are in one shout and all the hate like his is joined together and all the steps are moving, then who'll stand them?' He felt his way to his stool and the fire. 'It won't happen. No! That's the way of it. It never will.'

CHAPTER V

The flesh complains

I

When you get very old, your life at last runs broad and level and careless of its confines like a river spreading to meet the salt, illimitable sea. And when your eyes can mark no more the patient imperceptible change of light and season and year, the delight and sadness of face and gesture and even the withering of your own flesh, then you can only touch and listen; but mostly you wish to withdraw to the kindly lit world in your mind where the sight is never hurt and where the perturbing beat of time is heard faintly or not at all. Inside yourself you are awake in the way a man would be as he lies in bed after refreshing sleep. You lie still, knowing you are alert, enjoying the snugness that you have won for yourself from fret and worry. For why should a heart that will soon cease pulsing, break at the end by packing itself with anxiety or any mortal foolishness? The stars move and the sun crosses the heavens, and you can only wait till starshine and daylight pass from you for ever. But the body, so soon to fall to mealy clay, and the earth from which your clay was taken, will not leave the last serenity untouched. You must hunger; you must thirst; you must ache and be sick and shiver. Then you find yourself complaining bitterly that you are left neglected and your wants unattended, and that you are accounted almost as nothing among your own folk. You try to walk sturdily, drunk for a moment with pride in the strength that was yours in your youth, and your heart swells against your ribs and all your tired muscles and dry sinews protest with pain. You lie down, wondering dumbly at your body's defeat.

Those were the things that Donnacha Ruadh Mac Conmara strove to say in the days after the burning and the building and the coming of the man who had been lashed, but whatever he intended to utter changed on his lips to a fearful, querulous outcry.

When you get very old, you wish above all things to have your days flowing level and smooth... 'Why can't they leave the people alone? They took everything, land and wealth, and what can they want of beggars? Oh! why don't they leave us in our little peace? Why must they be lashing poor young lads and... our little peace, it's all we have.'

To see him sitting before the fire even on a warm summer's day, crouched and close-limbed over ashes and embers, was to feel winter creeping up your body like the swirl of a flood. With someone in the house, Eibhlín or Donnacha the son or a neighbour, he would grouse away on the stool, cackling at the humour of some saying that only himself understood, and when he was left alone he would whisper, shrug his lean shoulders into his coat, nestle down against foreboding and at last sit drooping and still. Tired of sitting he would feel his way to the door, sidle along the walls till he was out of the chill shadows, and then he would turn his head from side to side in the sunlight and face up at the sky, as if he were taking note of the weather and surveying the meadows and tree-lined river below. The unrest through which he had endeavoured to pass unperturbed had entered into him.

The men who came of nights gave up trying to turn him from complaining and from the fear that gripped him: fear of the final, complete destruction of all the people; but they did not know that what upset him in the remotest reaches of his soul, even unknown to himself, was the everpresent, wordless dread of inevitable death. Only in flashes, like the fire-spurts from kindling green wood, did he perceive what it was that unseated his repose, and in those flashes that brought fear like an acrid blinding smoke across his mind, he would think: Aye, I'm ready; I can die; I'll go to Purgatory at the worst for I had my pains on earth; and God's mercy and the prayers of my people will carry me the rest of the way; I can die indeed. But such resolute comforting could not quench terror. And so the men with whom he once gossiped and bragged found that he would tell no more tales nor give them snatches of verse nor, out of his learning, recount the wanderings of Odysseus and the heroes. There were other things to tell. When you get old and your course runs level and broad... 'Why can't they leave us our little peace?'

Only Eibhlín suffered him without a murmur. She gave him her care. For, the cherishing of a husband and of a house, the mothering and rearing of children, had fashioned and shaped her in such a way that, were she burdenless, she would be forlorn. The house was there: the blackened walls with the thatch weighed down with stones; the hearthstone for a fire; the table, the little dresser, the cupboard: all of it her house in which she moved deftly, feeding, washing, scraping, and in which she hoped to die. In it she had been loved and had borne children, and had watched over them with the sly, coaxing perseverance of her heart; and they had grown, so fast indeed that it seemed they walked out one day as children and returned in the evening and for a little while, grown full; then they were gone again, the floor was empty, and the hearth desolate. Her care she gave then to the scrawny bearded old man. She fed him when his fumbling fingers were impatient with the food; she washed him and combed and trimmed his beard; she helped him to dress and to undress, and drew the blankets about him when he lay down; and in the night when he grumbled at thirst or at hunger, she would arise without a word and give him drink or bread. 'Eibhlín, I'm thirsty... Eibhlín, give me a bit of bread... I'm cold, Eibhlín... There's a rent in my coat... Where's my stick?... Bring me the stool... Hurry, woman.' She did not complain.

II

She was glad when, at the time of the haymaking, the soldiers were billeted over in Ardone at the western end of the valley. The old man would have something now to bother the neighbours with in the night.

'Listen, men,' said he, 'I don't know whether you notice it or not. Maybe you were born too late. Men, the world is going mad with wickedness. There is more between the gentry and the soldiers and the government-men than we know. Look! I was down at the sea and soldiers came and flogged a man. And there was a young gentleman named... What was his name? God bless this sieve of a head, for it holds nothing now! And look, I came here to Knockanee and what did I see? The houses of the people in flames and women crying out their hearts over the little things lost. And the other day a man walks into this house with his back lashed. Every other day we get stories and rumours. One half of them may be lies, but the other half is enough. Floggings, beatings, burnings, with soldiers living on the people, demanding the best of everything, paying for nothing, threatening the men and ill-treating the women. They kick us like dogs that have neither teeth nor claws. Dogs, mangy dogs, that's what we are.

'But let you listen. I know what's afoot.

'Do you know, men, what they want us to do? They want us to strike back. They want us to show fight. And the very minute we lift our heads and stir a hand, they'll be down on top of us with horses and guns and there won't be left a man alive or free, or a woman safe, or a house standing with a roof.

'Look, men. I've seen many a year of hunger and many a year of plenty, and I've seen many a year of peace and many a year of trouble. I thought that, as time passed, the hatred of the gentry for us and our children would die away. We pay rents. We pay tithes. We give them our sweat. They do with us as they please. But what is it, in the name of God Almighty, that they want of us now?

'Why don't they leave us our little peace?'

They did not answer but, with heads bent, stared at their brown gnarled clasped hands or tapped a toe on the ground and hummed a tune. What was the use of answering? Guns and horses had not yet come, and if they were to come, let them. What was the use of trying to change the wind or to beat back the water of the river?

III

Donnacha the son took him down in a cart to the long river-side meadow on one of the days when Mr. Dundee's hay was being cut. He put him under an elm where the sunshine was a wavering veil of golden flecks on the generous shadow and there left him sitting at his ease.

They said it was a warm summer, as warm as they could recall. In some places the wheat had already turned. The river was low and weedy, and the boys could go barefoot in the pools or lie on their bellies on the banks to tickle trout.

It was pleasant under the tree after the winter and the spring in the house. There were three scythemen in the meadow, Donnacha amongst them, paying off arrears of rent. As they came near the elm, the old man could hear the swish, bite and dim song-song of their blades, and as they passed, sweating, heads down, knees bent, shoulders swaying, he would jeer them to his heart's content, telling them that in his time one man could do the work of the three of them put together and before his dinner.

They let him draw them and he heard one say as blades were being honed: 'It's good, Donnacha, to see him so happy.'

And another added: 'The winter is hard on the old.'

Then, the son's murmur: 'His heart is up one day and down another. That's the way we'll all go.'

Sometimes they would pause to reply to his badgering, and instantly he would charge them with idling and with seeking after an excuse for a rest because the work had beaten them flat. What kind of men were they who couldn't work under a sun that was no stronger than the heat of a spring day? Yet the sun was strong upon him and he dozed, still hearing the tiny hum of the blades and pretending not to hear the words the men flung at him to keep his heart glad. Drowsily he heeded their talk when they came and sat beside him in the shade for a rest, slow talk that weighed his mind with sleep and made the eyelids too heavy to rise.

'What's Mr. Dundee doing with himself at all these days?'

'God help him, the poor man.'

'He goes around like a man who's lost. I saw him standing and staring at the river the other day for fully half an hour.'

'It's his river anyway. The yardboy told me he sits up till all hours, with three or four candles lit. He doesn't have any company now either.'

'I wonder was it true about breaking the glasses and bottles?'

'Is it about the night he was drinking and shouting against the government? I don't believe a word of it. That story was put around to harm him.'

'Well, the yard boys in the loft heard him.'

'Ah, well it's not our business. There's nobody like him as a landlord anyway.'

'Aye! Lord God, it's warm.'

And at noon, while the scythemen were working, Dundee himself rode by along the bank of the river and the men, calling out good-day across the levelled swathes, awakened Donnacha Ruadh. He heard Dundee, nearby, replying gruffly, and then adding in English, 'You are taking the sun, I see. Please do not get up. You're as good a man as I am. Isn't that true?'

Hastily Donnacha Ruadh said, 'It's a great day, sir. The hay's in fine condition.'

'You, I'm told, are a wise man. Are you? What would you do if you were in my shoes?'

'I don't understand you, sir, Mr. Dundee.'

'Ha! then you are not a prophet outside your own house. You were never in Dublin, were you? There is a city of prophets. They speak, nay, they whisper, and behold! a man they never saw is taken from his house and chastised for the good of the people, the peace of the realm, and in honour of his glorious majesty. Prophesy, man. Are you a Jeremias or merely a Job? You do not know, sir. Would you like to be a Frenchman?'

86

'I wouldn't like to be a king of the Frenchmen, sir.'

Dundee laughed dryly. 'You fancy,' said he, 'that I'm baiting you.' He laughed again. 'Yes, we must be wary in these times. But they'll never catch old birds with chaff, will they, my friend? We're old birds, you and I?'

'Aye, there are snares, sir.'

'The prophet speaks. Spoken like a true prophet. Snares? Good-day.'

After Dundee had gone, the scythemen gathered in haste under the elm but all their wheedling and begging could not get from Donnacha Ruadh one word of what had been said.

'I don't know, men,' he murmured. 'Honest to God, I didn't understand the man. He has a burden on him. He's sick. He's in torment.'

'He's one of the few good landlords who ever lived,' said a scytheman.

And Donnacha Ruadh added, 'His own will crucify him.' Then he muttered, 'What's wrong with him? He was talking like a... like a... Leave me alone men and don't be bothering me. O leave me alone.'

They left him sitting against the tree and there he stayed, carrying on a quiet conversation with himself, while the shade in which he rested slipped from beneath him as the sun swung down the heavens. Soon the rays slanted in a blaze on his head, pierced through his clothes and into his flesh so that, under the heat, a thin perspiration moistened his back and neck. The fibres of his clothes irritated his skin but he was too drowsy to move after the creeping shade of the foliage. Uneasiness, like faint nausea, crept through him. Of a sudden, so that he thought for the instant that a cloud obscured the sun, his body became cool, and his hearing and his touch and his smell became wonderfully acute. The sun still beat upon his head. He could almost scent the beams. Beneath his fingers he could feel the dampishly cool grass, the roughness of its edges, the ribs in the tiny pointed blades; and an insect crawling amongst the hairs on his calloused hands had every fraction of its passage noted. His back knew the wrinkles and curves of the tree against which he leaned and a rustling, strangely insistent, showered down upon his hearing from the massed leaves overhead. The scent of the hay almost stifled him, and on every slight puff of wind he caught a weedy sweet odour from the river. Out on the meadow the scythes were whining finely and the men murmuring. From all around him sounds streamed in; a dog barking; water swishing around the rock in a pool; no bird still in any place; a cart rattling; a man halooing a horse; and a girl singing on the hillside. For a moment, for the space of a few breaths, he was exalted. Then his flesh seemed to turn; and across his soul, like a cloud-shadow winging darkly across tautly surfaced water, there swept the thought of the passing of all things. And he was falling, his heart pounding, his bowels writhing to a retch. He dug his crooked fingers into the sod on each side for support, but still sliding down, soundlessly and into a gathering dark. In that dark his eyes, he thought, were healed and opened and they saw flames spitting like whip-lashes, the contorted faces of women made hags by terror, men running aimlessly and glancing over their hunched shoulders, a boy kicking at the end of a turning rope slung from a great tree, and the whole world, the fields and hills and houses, even the high sky, were choking in smoke. Against the fall he struck out desperately, against the featureless dark that was mawing up everything, and for a second he regained his senses. His stomach was heaving. His mouth was bitter. Perspiration was cooling on his back and brow. Suddenly, thinking that this was death, he yielded and he was claimed by an abyss.

Late in the evening the scythemen, calling on him to wake up, walked to the elm to bring him home.

They knelt when he did not stir, felt his pulse, listened to his heart and lifted his eyelids.

'It was the strong sun,' said one of the men.

Two of them lifted him between them while the third ran for a cart.

IV

He could not tell whether he was standing or lying. It was like the day of his boyhood when, diving in the Shannon, he became entangled in weeds with which he struggled in a yellowish greenish light full of indefinite shadows and trailing vegetation. He knew that if he remained quiet just for a moment and controlled his limbs, he would slip free and rise to the surface to fill his aching burning chest with air but he could not suppress the fear that made him mad. The drumming was in his ears, the throbbing in his blood, the murky light in his eyes, and he was suffocating.

He braced himself against the fear. The drumming and the throbbing left him, and in the calmness he could see. He was sure he could see. The glow on the people was smoky, like the sunshine seen through a bottle, but he was sure they were real people.

What were they doing all around him? Donnacha his son, and Máire his wife, and Máire his daughter; their children; an old priest in a great soutane walking round and round a splashing glittering fountain in a Roman courtyard; his father and mother, shaking his hand. He laughed. Why, the old couple must be as old as the hills! They were all talking to him and he was answering back, whipping them to laughter with his replies, but two women of them, Máire his wife and Máire his daughter, stared at him with pale, lovely but accusing faces. He must tell them all about the things he had seen and done and about how he slowly lost his sight and got it back again. That would make them glad, all of them, all those people who passed behind his own kin in a procession. He must tell them. He struggled. He was rising and the light was changing, and he was floating into a tremorless sleep.

Again, clear but low, voices were about him. He recognised them. Eibhlín and Donnacha were talking.

'He'll have to be very careful, Eibhlín, from this day out. It was touch and go with him.'

'I'm worn out anyway. Day after day I was sure he was breathing his last.'

'The priest thought it too. Woman, he's as hard to kill as a rock from the mountain.'

'Look! he's lying quiet. He's breathing at his ease. O thanks be to God, the poor old man, hasn't he suffered enough?'

The voices were nearer. Damn the woman anyway. Why was she crying? Women were always whingeing. He'd take a sleep, a short nap and then tell her not to be foolish. He would say to her that tears never...

It seemed to him that he had been asleep only a minute and that the warmth of the bed and the heaviness of the clothes had awakened him. He wanted to scratch his head but his arm appeared to be remote and refused to move no matter how much he wished. His tongue was thick, furry, foul. He called the woman's name.

'Eibhlín! Eibhlín!'

'Yes.'

'Eibhlín, come here. Eibhlín. Woman.'

'Yes. I'm here.'

'Speak up.'

'I'm listening, father.'

'Was Máire here? Máire?'

'Who?'

'Máire. My own Máire?'

'God shield us, he's...'

'Máire my daughter?'

'Nor she either. Rest yourself, father. Would you like a drink?'

'Aye! Aye! But are you sure, woman?'

'I'm sure.'

'My daughter wasn't here? You're sure?'

'Nobody was here for the past week but a few neighbours and a man from Lacken House. Wait now and I'll give you a drop of Mr. Dundee's wine.'

'Wine?' He licked his lips and felt that his tongue was caked with clay.

Her arm, lifting him up in the bed, was hard beneath his shoulders and the palm of her hand was cold. A spoon was against his mouth. He sipped, sighed and opened his mouth for more, sipped again and began to chuckle. She put a cup against his lips and he held on to it, fingering it impatiently, even when he had drained the last drop. He lay down smiling.

'What time of day is it, Eibhlín?'

'Morning, and what else?'

The smile left his face and his eyes moved vainly in their sockets: 'Is the sun shining?'

'It is. Sleep now.'

'The sun is shining.' He moaned. 'The sun. Where are all the people gone?'

V

He had to keep to the bed all the time when the corn was ripening and being reaped and while the hillsides were becoming brown and the trees in the valley flecked with rust. Yet, as if his body were part of the corn and the trees, changing as they changed, he missed none of the turning season. The turn was in the air, in the early morning chill and the long, stealthy evening; and he knew it from the gabble of the harvesting people who came to see him of nights and then to gossip, leaving him silent and almost forgotten on his bed. He did not mind the silence now nor the forgetfulness. There was much to remember.

On the day Eibhlín went with other women to pick and store in the barn the apples in Lacken orchard, he was left alone and dressed on the bed with his stick out of reach lest he should wander. He had wanted to go too. She would come home with a bag of windfall apples for herself; and her quiet talk, without envy, would be about the good harvest, the full barn, the food they ate at the House, and the piles of red and bright green fruit that would be pressed for cider. He wanted to look on, to feel the plentiful crops that were, like a needed blessing, so comforting and so assuring of God's generous hand. And he was weary of the smell of smoke in the small kitchen, the tang of ashes, and of the steam of water bubbling around potatoes, and of the damp clay of the floor and walls. Maybe she would bring him if he asked her again.

There were footsteps on the stones outside the door.

'Is that you, Eibhlín? Are you back so soon?'

He sat up with a great effort when he got no answer.

'Donnacha, is that yourself? I'm hungry.'

Bare knuckles were rapped on the open door.

'Who's that?'

'God save all here,' was the reply. The voice was deep and chesty.

'Who are you?'

'Is this the house of Donnacha Mac Conmara?'

'If you're a stranger, what do you want?'

'That's a fine welcome to my father's house, if it is my father's house.'

'Your father?'

'I'm Mícheál.'

Donnacha Ruadh lifted himself from the edge of the bed and stood. 'Step here, lad,' said he. 'Step here. Come in, in. It's your father's house. Your mother will break her heart for seeing you.' He walked a pace, tottered, and arms hard with muscle and unyielding like boughs, held him up. He set his feet firmly on the floor. 'The old legs, they're unwilling. Here, let me see you.' He felt with his hand along the shoulders to the face and his fingers measured the set mouth, the nose with the high bridge, the brows and the broad forehead. 'Don't you know me at all, lad. You have my face, don't you know that? Hah! you have my hard face. Your mother will cry herself sick. Ah! but you're tall. I was tall once too. Why didn't you come home sooner? You're a rogue like your grandfather, a wandering rogue like your grandfather. I'm on my last legs, lad. I was like you once. Put me back on the bed. I haven't a breath left. There, throw me down. You're your grandfather all right.'

Mícheál was laughing easily and softly. He said, 'That was a fine welcome you gave me when I came to the door.'

'But, man, didn't I make up for it? Where have you been at all, Michéal? You'll stay now, won't you? One wanderer is enough in a family. Your father's not a young man and your mother is not a young woman. You'll stay. To be sure you will. Just like myself you are: nobody knows when you'll come, when you'll go.'

'Where's my mother?'

'Down at Lacken House.'

'Working?'

'Aye.'

'Paying rent?'

'Aye, son. So she is.'

Michéal plumped down on a stool, blew out his breath in a soundless whistle, and tapped on the hearthstone with the toes of his shoes. Suddenly he said, 'I'm not staying. I am not.'

'Ah! Michéal, Michéal, and you only after coming home! It'll kill her.'

'I'm going away. Across the sea. What in the name of God is there in all Ireland for the son of a man like...'

'This house and the bit of land are there for you, I'm sure, lad.'

'The bit of land and the house, and my mother killing herself down in Lacken!'

'Better men had less, lad.'

'Is it to sweat for rent and tithes and to hang my head before the men who'll take my money? By God, I will not, grandfather. I'm as good a man as they are. We were all born of women. I'll go where I can talk to any man as to a neighbour. Look here. Listen to me.' He was up lithely on his feet, over beside the bed, clamping his fist into his palm, and tat-tatting out all that was in his heart like musketry fire. 'I'm young. I'm strong. I have a head. I'm willing to sweat. Aye, I thank God for His gifts. But, by the high and living...'

'But your mother and father, son?'

'All right! My mother! My father! I've been over half Ireland. I worked in the fields of the gentry. I worked in the stables of the gentry. I ate the bite that was flung to me. I worked in the towns. In Dublin I was hungry, where the streets are crawling with poor men begging. O, the big men have their fine houses and their demesnes and their finery and their straps. But grandfather, my God, grandfather, what is there for the likes of me?

'Do you know what they do now? Are you so asleep with old age that you can't see? They flog men. They destroy the women and the young girls. They put soldiers in the houses. I saw it. I saw it with these eyes in Wexford, in a village. They're trying to wipe out the whole Irish breed, the whole cowardly godforsaken lickspittle breed. What is there for the likes of me, will you tell me? Fight, is it? To have my guts torn out for the dogs while the rest looked on? I don't know how on God's earth you and all the old people, aye, my father and mother, didn't pack their bundles and run to the ships to get away forever, you and your kind and their sons.'

Mícheál paused, breathing strongly through his nostrils, and his tenseness eased itself so that he seated himself again.

'You'd think,' Donnacha Ruadh mused, 'that it was myself who spoke, and I young and red with anger.'

'Well, I'm going. Nobody will stop me. I have a little money saved and I'll be in Waterford again in a week. There's a ship sailing to America.'

'Your mother won't begrudge it to you, son.'

At mention of his mother, the young man sighed and next spoke into his hands with which he supported his head.

'Grandfather,' said he, 'I saw my aunt, Máire, and your grandchildren in Kilmacthomas. They're all well. Yes, they're well. She said that if ever I should lay my eye on you, I was to give you this message: that you're welcome to her house.' He chuckled, as he added, 'But you're to go to her before you die.'

The toothless mouth laughed soundlessly up at the low hanging wisps of the roof.

VI

They heard her coming when the evening was grey. She was home before her husband, her day's work done. She trudged to the door, stooping under a sack of apples, and the bundle of sticks and brosna she had foraged on her way from the ditches below. Outside the threshold, she swung down her bundle and her bag, released back her shoulders with a gasp, and then, with the knuckles of her hands, stroked the perspiration and the rat-tails of hair from her forehead. She halted, her hands clasped and against her mouth, and thus remained, listening, caught in the momentary brooding that comes upon women and mercifully removes them from the world: along the river a sheepdog was barking busily and a man whistling at cattle knee-deep in the water. Dully she asked, 'Are you all right, father?'

Her son was standing and facing the door, his head bent from the sooty trailings of thatch above the hearth.

She saw him. Fearfully she moved towards him. He held her shoulders, leaned down, and swiftly kissed her head. She pulled away, at once all full of care and the thought of preparing a meal, and as she reached toward the embers of the fire with a rushlight, she glanced up at him, unbelieving. Of a sudden she swept the light up before his face and stared.

'It is Michéal,' she said slowly.

Then her tongue wagged. With her rapid deft short steps she pattered to the dresser, took two stumps of tallow-candles from a box, lit them, and with her shaking hands jiggling the flames, set the lights standing in wax droppings on the bare boards of the table. On and on she talked: 'Sit down Michéal. You must be starving, son. You must be tired. I'll have supper ready. Pull in to the fire, son. It gets chill these evenings. The harvest was grand. I must put a patch on that coat of yours. You're looking fine, son...'

Donnacha Ruadh was sitting up on the edge of the bed with something like a song stirring his mind for this woman who, he could sense, was ready to unloose joy that would seem too like insuppressible grief, so racking would it be, so loud with uncontrolled cries, so like the outburst of a heart that found the fulfilment of a long-held desire at last and with high overwhelming surprise.

'I always said,' he murmured, 'and I say it now, that we always found women too good for us.'

CHAPTER VI

Consuming fire

I

Donnacha Ruadh turned himself slowly on his side, thereby rustling the straw in the thin tick, and lifted himself on his hands to hear better. The coverlet fell from his shoulder so that he felt the night draughts cold on his bared chest. He had not been mistaken, he assured himself. The snuffling, throat-caught sobbing he had heard was not a trick of his sleepless mind recalling old things. She, Eibhlín, was crying, alone over in the corner in the darkness.

He held himself on his trembling arms. A tiny piece of green wood, brushed up with the banked embers on the hearth, was spewing steaming sap. Wind sighed against the hillside. She still wept. He nodded his head. A kind word, he knew, to a worrying woman, would release tears and loud, protesting wailing. But he could not say a harsh word. For who could blame her?

The son, departed these three days for Waterford, had gone gladly and eagerly to reside among strangers, to work and rear a family and then die across the sea, unknown to his people at home, a stranger for ever. The father, neither commending nor condemning, had accompanied him. He, Donnacha Ruadh, had desired to go too so that the two men could leave him on their way safely with his daughter in Kilmacthomas where he could die as he wished. They would not let him. Too ill he was, they told him; and besides, what would Eibhlín do alone without him? He pleaded with them, begging for that one favour, the last they could ever give him, but they would not. They would not take a chance with him, and he weak enough to breathe his last under the hardship of the road, and so they went.

His arms weakening under the weight of his body, he let himself down again to the tick and as he did so, he knocked over a mug of water that stood beside his head on a stool. Instantly, Eibhlín ceased crying. He heard her sitting up.

'Are you all right, father?' she inquired anxiously. How many times had she not asked that question since he came beneath the roof! He tried to lie still where he was. She asked again. Then, he could not help saying what he said.

'Hush, woman. They come and they go as if they never had a mother or father at all. They are with you one day, weighing you down with trouble and giving you joy that they never know till their own turn comes, and then they leave you the next day and your house empty. That's why you were born; for that you were made. You're a woman. Sleep now.'

He thought she was stretching quiet then, for her breathing, except for a little occasional shiver in it, was regular. When she spoke he surmised that she was sitting up, wide-eyed and awake, maybe staring at the red pinched glow of the fire. She said:

'He was a fine lad. In truth, they were all good children and I could never say a thing against them. I think it was better for him to go.'

'Sure it was, Eibhlín. You don't know how fortunate he is to be leaving a land where the best men must be content with the scraps thrown by the rich. An old man, it's true, could be content like that, but to a young heart it's unjust. It's not natural. And besides, he could easily have got himself into trouble with the soldiers or these United men. Now, do you remember that young lad who walked over the hills with the flesh on his back...'

'Almighty God,' she said once, tonelessly.

'Even the gentry themselves have to be careful, daughter, and when they must walk warily what chance is there for a young lad whose heart is hot and angry? Look at poor Mr. Dundee. They say his own rank hate him because... Don't let me talk. Sleep, woman.'

She did not lie down. In a burst she said, 'Don't let you go away now. You'll be with Máire, your daughter, time enough. You have the years before you yet.'

'The years?' he said. He lay on his back, pulled up the coverlet as if it were a pall, to his bearded chin, and shuddered.

'Don't go from us,' she repeated.

'No!' he murmured.

But his mind was made up. He would go before Christmas before the roads ran like dykes with the floods, and down in his daughter's house with his grandchildren he would squeeze out what merriment and laughter he could, and he would say his prayers in the quietness like the quietness of a wood in the autumn when death comes kindly. If he could not go before the Christmas, then he would make the journey in the spring, and no weather, no son, no woman's pleading, would hinder him. He would get inside his daughter's house to shelter himself from the bleak unwholesome wind that blew across a world where men talked all night long of pain and the whip and spilling blood and the French and ships and war, and never once of the lords that were gone or of the old songs or the ancient books. Down in her house, unmolested, he would live as he lived in that happy time when... he sought this way and that in his memory for those days that fell across his darkling course like a strong unblemished sunbeam, and for all his searching he could not discover the lost, clear warm days. Yet, they must have happened. He could feel the mellow ruddy glow of them even now in his heart, but why that glow was there, whence he had recollected it, he could not tell; and to comfort himself he said that it was a light beyond the edge of the world, a day sunken for ever below the horizon: a joy given and gone before he was born. Nourished and soothed, he slept.

When he awoke he heard Eibhlín stirring and scraping among the ashes of the fire. He sat up. Smoke was thin on the air.

'Is it the day?' he asked.

'I can't sleep. Lie easy, yourself. I'll be all right. I'll be all right in a few days.'

'It's a shame for you at your age to be taking loss like that. But I know you. You'll not be right till you're dead.'

'The weather's turning. It's bitter cold, father.'

I I

The evening Donnacha Óg returned from seeing his son away, he, tired as he was, set about finishing the digging out of the potatoes under the little light there was left to the short day. 'We'll have to put them in the pits against the frost as soon as we can,' he explained.

'Have you any news of Máire?' the father asked.

'I must be busy. Some other time.'

The father recognised the excuse for what it was. Hard as this man seemed, so unfeeling and gruff and distrustful of any show of sorrow or joy, yet he was, the old man perceived, as inwardly shaken by the departure of Micheál as though death had struck. He was certain that on some quay in Waterford or in some poor tavern where they had bedded for the night, there had passed between the two of them, the father and the son, some kind of speech, a few half-said words about nothing at all and about the grief of the mother, and that once they had spoken thus they would utter no other word.

'Well,' said Donnacha Ruadh again in the night, 'what's the

news of Máire? Is she well? Did she inquire after me?'

'She's in the best of health, and she did talk about you.'

'Whisper. Don't let Eibhlín hear. When am I to go and live in Kilmacthomas?'

'Put it out of your mind for a while,' the son rasped. 'You're welcome any time you go there. Why is it, father, that all your life you're restless in the one place? You'd hardly stay in heaven.'

He was not to be put off with an answer like that. He would find his chance. He only half-listened to the stories and rumours his son had gathered on the road between Kilmacthomas and Waterford, stories that neighbours waited for with, as Eibhlín remarked, their tongues hanging out like hounds around a slaughterhouse. The father and Mícheál slept one night under the hayrick of a big house where there was a party and dancing, and all the night carriages with lamps were coming and going up to the rows of lighted windows, and women with fine dresses were chattering and laughing and men were staggering around drunk; and at midnight a group of young fellows came out to the stables to take horses and to ride mad across the fields in the dark and to fire off pistols at a scarecrow which, they declared, was a United man. But if there was merriment in the big houses, there was dread in the little ones of the people. Even wherever the soldiers had not been, there was terror of them, and every man kept his tongue quiet lest his neighbour should be either a tale-bearer or a United man, either of whom could bring trouble. Everywhere the people said that it could not last because flesh and blood could not endure suffering for ever. In the city, in the tavern in Waterford, there were a few townsmen, talkative but suspicious of everybody, who expected fighting of some sort to break out in those townlands and villages where men had been flogged, girls and women destroyed, cattle driven away and houses burned to the foundations. One man was willing to wager a silver watch that the day a chapel would be burned there would be bloody and immediate war; because then the patience of the restraining priests would be gone. Yes! there were plenty of ships, to be sure, along the quays in Waterford, a good number of them from the Land of the Fish; the shops were busy; the streets were full of carts: but he, Donnacha Óg, had not paid much attention.

'Well, men,' said Donnacha Ruadh before the neighbours, 'I can't have much longer to live, but I hope and trust in God that I'll never see the day when the people run crazy for killing. Anyway, I don't think any of us will see it. They'll lie down and let it pass, like a man shielding himself on the ground from racing horses.'

'Faith then,' said a neighbour, spitting defiantly in the fire and jogging his head confidently, 'they'll not lie down here in a hurry.' No one heeded him because he was a braggart.

'I'll not be here long either,' continued Donnacha Ruadh. 'My son will be taking me down to the house of my own daughter in a few weeks, or shortly after Christmas. Isn't that true, son? You can't deny it. You're all witnesses to it.'

'Listen,' said the son hotly, 'is it shaming me before the parish you are? You know right well I never mentioned a word of the kind. You old fox.'

'You did. Oh! indeed you did, son. Now, son, you did.'

'You're hearing more than is said these days.'

III

Whatever the cause, whether it was the return of the season of the burning or whether it was the news that Donnacha Óg picked up on the road, foreboding settled on the minds of the people. There was no night they sat down beside their fires, crouching closer as the frosts or winds sharpened outside, but they asked somewhere in their talk: What'll we do if the soldiers come down on us again? How can we bear it if the houses are given to the flames over our heads? From their doors and from the slanting fields they watched by day, and spied, almost unknown to themselves, on the distant strips of road and mountain path. Along some of those ways, they feared, the red-coated white-breeched devils would come, and then there would be drum-beats, the lash, the flames again, and maybe the rope on a tree beside the river.

Coming on towards the Christmas they were roused from their beds one grey morning by a shouting boy who ran along the narrow paths and clambered over walls in a skelter. 'Mr. Dundee is shot,' he cried, banging on some doors, calling through tiny windows. There was a ring in the echoes of his voice like the burden of a lonely bell. 'Mr. Dun-n-n-dee is shot.'

Donnacha Ruadh was the first in his son's house to hear the cry and, trying to disentangle the echoes from the vague swirl of dreams and memories that had foamed through his shallow sleep, he crawled on his hands and knees to awaken his son.

'O God,' said Eibhlín, hearing the babble of cries, 'is it the fire again? The soldiers, is it?'

The son was silent as he dressed.

Dogs were barking then and in a few houses very young children were crying out in fear and women were hushing them. Donnacha Óg went at a half-trot down the valley along which, motionless, white and trailing in flocks, lay mist awaiting the weak sun. He beat his hands together against the cold. The cocks were crowing forlornly.

In Lacken House many windows in the front were lit with candles that flickered erratically within, warm to the chill greyness of the dawn, as servants and yardmen hastened through the rooms and banged doors and pounded up and down the stairways. A stableboy, swinging a lighted lantern, ran up the drive from the shrubbery and would not delay for one instant to speak to the gathering men from the farms, but pushed them off and disappeared into the house.

Donnacha Óg found himself growling out anger with the others on the steps beneath the portico. Like himself they had come hurriedly. A few were entirely barefoot, hatless and clad only in breeches and shirt, and these, trying to warm their freezing knuckles under their oxters, shifted and danced and fidgeted; while others, with great coats and blankets across their shoulders, stood still and chattered all together. What happened? Who did it? Was it shooting? Was it a duel? Did Mr. Dundee ever challenge a man? By the Lord, won't we take whoever did it and tear him limb from limb? What did the boy say? They were shouting questions and advice in a confusion that carried far over the dawn-quiet valley when the housekeeper suddenly opened the front door and said: 'Hold your tongues, people. Noise is no cure for a sick man. You're to go home.' She banged the door then against the crush of their bodies.

But they would not go home. They hung about the steps, sitting on the stone and getting up restlessly, staring at the twin iron lion-heads at each side of the door, shivering, mumbling, calling down great oaths to emphasize that although Dundee was one of the gentry, he had been good to them from the first day he put a foot on the land. By and by, as shadows took definite shape on the shaggy lawns and as walls reflected the rose-light blooming in the east, the women arrived in twos and threes, nodding their heads together to the tune of wagging tongues, and they grouped and stood apart under a tree at the grass-edge. All the men were hungry by that time and numbed to the heart. In desperation they seized the stableboy who had passed into the house with the lantern and who now emerged straight into their hands, chewing at a hunk of cold beef. From him they got the story after pelting him with more questions than he could hear. One man threatened to knock his teeth down his throat if he didn't speak promptly.

Mr. Dundee had gone on a visit the night before to the big house three miles east of Lacken where certain gentlemen, a parliament man and two ministers were waiting for him. The stableboy had gone riding, too, with the lantern, and it was of what he had overheard from the dining-room and from the gossip of servants, that he fashioned his tale.

'They were,' said he, 'quiet and sober at first, drinking their claret and brandy and rum that the servants were tired carrying around. Soon loud grand lathery talk began and it was all for the master's benefit. It was about the stories going the rounds: how he had treated the officer and the soldiers; how lax he was with his tenants, that is, yourselves; and how bad was the example he was setting. They were talking to him, they said, for his own good, and they didn't intend any offence because they were all friends. And Ben – Ben is the headservant over there – went into the room in the middle of this with bottles as his excuse for picking up a word or two. He felt all the pity in the world for the poor master, Mr. Dundee, who is always kind and considerate with his purse wherever he goes. There was Mr. Dundee sitting at one side of a fine table with his glass untasted before him and he sitting like a statue; only his eyes were going from face to face. You know the way he examines you when anything is wrong. A minister was giving out at that minute about the danger of the Frenchmen who had been kept away from Ireland only by God's providence and he laid it down like a law that it was no occasion for any gentleman to be lax in anything and that they'd all have to show how loyal they were to the government and the Crown and their own kind.

'Ben was ordered to leave the room then and not to return next or nigh the place unless he was sent for. He went but he stayed outside, near the door. He said it was a shame the way they spoke up to the master who never showed any sign of anger or impatience. That's what Ben said. But he doesn't know the master.

'The anger must have been working there in him all the time till it was like a hound in leash. It was let go. It was let go and no lie. Every soul in the house must have heard the first roar, like a bull's, and then a chair going over and after that all the glasses and bottles rolling to the floor and jingling and smashing. There they were, all against him, and he caught the table and turned it over on top of them and called them savages and

101

lickspittles and the scum of the country. I saw one of them myself, a minister, galloping full belt down the stairs with his arms waving, and out of the house with him, saying, "God bless my soul, a lunatic." Someone in the room had a pistol primed and ready. More than one in that room had a pistol. Maybe it was the master himself. Ben, the headman, swears it was the master who pulled out a pistol. Then a shot went off, and then another fit to split your ears. The next thing the door opened again and here was the master coming down the stairs, holding on to the banisters, with blood pouring down his forehead and over his eyes. "Get me Jane," says he. "This is no house for Christian or heathen. Footpads!" Those were his words. I saddled Jane and by the time I got him into the saddle he had a towel around his head and he was as pale as death and woefully silent. I brought him home safe, thank God. There's my story, men. He's alright. The ball only grazed the top of his head. Another bit, men, just the width of my nail, and I tell you he'd have come home on a cart.'

Dazed with the cold, Donnacha Óg went home in the full morning to his own hearth over which he held himself close. His father was breaking fast on a bowl of oatmeal.

'Where's my woman, father? There's nothing much wrong down in Lacken.'

'She's down at a neighbour's. A child took sick with fright. A man was here, a travelling-man.'

'What man at this hour?'

'He had a message for you.'

'For me? Are you dreaming?'

'From your sister. You're to send me home to her without delay. Those were the words. That's the message. Now, tell me what happened at Lacken?'

'I said nothing much. Now, wasn't it a queer hour for travelling-men who are not given to listening to the cocks?'

'So it was, son. Aye, that's true.'

'Was Eibhlín here when he was telling you all that?'

'I couldn't tell you exactly, son. This porridge is all lumps. Have your own from the pot.'

'Was Eibhlín here? Yes or no?'

'Son, how could a poor blind man like me see? Don't be hard on me, Donnacha.'

It was the New Year before Mr. Dundee was fit to ride around among the people of Knockanee and the farms in the valley. He was muffled up in a long black surcoat with his billycock hat well down on his head, so that he appeared more like a priest riding out in the parish than a landlord. Like a priest they met him. One man led his horse by the bridle and a group of men followed behind everywhere he went. They would not allow Dundee to dismount but called out the people from the houses for a word, a wan smile, an inquiry about rent or a sick child. All of them noted that on the face of this man, pallid and splotched with purple veins, there was a look of abstraction they had never observed before.

At the house of Donnacha Mac Conmara who was himself down at Lacken building a wall with other men, there was no one at home except Eibhlín who hardly lifted her eyes for shyness, and the old man who clung to the jamb of the door, thrusting his beard forward curiously and chewing like a goat. Dundee smiled.

'Ha! Here's our old warrior,' said he. 'You're still alive.'

'Alive? I'll outlive you all, so I will.'

Dundee's laugh put them at their ease and for courtesy they all laughed quietly.

'I'm sure you will. I hope you will,' said Dundee. 'In truth, I think you could surpass most of the young men.'

'Young men? Bah! they're not rearing them now. There's that young son of mine!' A titter went round. Dundee raised his whip-hand to his lips. 'I hear, sir, that they tried to blow your brains out. They couldn't blow the like out of any of the men standing around here, or the women either. Empty-skulls, jeering old men like myself.'

'I'm glad,' Dundee said, 'you're in such good health. I don't suppose you have a care or a discontent in the world. When the mind is free...'

'No, no, sir, not a care, thank you,' Eibhlín interrupted.

'I have then,' said Donnacha Ruadh, moving closer to the horse. 'Sir, I have a daughter, sir, and it's living with her I should be now. She's a fine young woman, but this son of mine wouldn't bother his head about bringing me down to her house. Now, is that just or proper in my own flesh and blood? Did you... Now what am I... If there was...' He spluttered and waved his stick so that the man at the bridle was almost lifted into the air by the shying, uprearing horse.

'That's not my business,' Dundee replied. 'Dammit, keep your stick quiet.'

Eibhlín caught Donnacha Ruadh around the shoulders while other women joined to give her help and between them they pushed and sidled the old muttering man back into the house where he stood, stooped, his fingers clawing, and told them in a rush of words of which they could catch only a few that it was a shame and a disgrace to treat him like that and he conversing with a gentleman.

'Get out of this house,' he said. 'You're nothing but straps to be pestering me. Go and roll in the ditches with your young fools of lads. Get out. I tell you, I'll go from cursed Knockanee on my hands and knees like a dog, if I have to do it.'

They left himself and Eibhlín alone. She pulled her shawl around her shoulders resolutely and whitefaced, turned to him. 'I never thought,' she reproached, 'that you'd do such a thing before half the parish. O father, why did you do it? You know that my man will do as you wish when he can – when – you're well.'

'When I'm well?'

'Look at yourself now. Like an empty sack. There, sit down on the bed. O why did you do it at all?'

He held her hand between his own two trembling paws and patted it awkwardly. When his breathing became calmer and fitted for measured words, he spoke to her. Stonily and haltingly he spoke as though he repeated a litany that the tongue and mouth could shape without direction from the mind: a litany that the flesh bore familiarly like the scars of old, grave wounds.

'I had a family, woman. You have the son. He's a good man. A good man took the daughter. It was to her I gave the best of my affection. Indeed, woman, she was like her mother. In her house I'd rather die than anywhere on earth. You and I and God know that I can't have much longer to live. I'm tired of travelling and wandering like a rudderless boat. I'm tired of thinking whether there's yet another house in which a travelling-man would be welcome. There's not much left to me now. What good are my books and I blind and forgetful? Once I made verse. Not even that now! Aye, I'm failing. My wife lies where my daughter lives. I'd like to put my bones in that place, in that yard, in that clay. Whisht, daughter.'

The dark days were going unregretted. The earth felt the change in clay and root, in running water and creeping thing and flying fowl. There was not one soul in Knockanee who did not exult, bij word or gesture or look, over passing unscathed through the purgatorial distress and terror of the winter. Three great blessings they counted: neither the soldiers nor the yeomanry had ridden upon them; the houses were standing safe; and there had been no death. Hearts could well rejoice when, on the Sunday that brought sunshine falling flawlessly in cascades through the little windows of the chapel, the priest unvested to preach and to thank God for the blessings, and exultation was confirmed.

They could work now for a good year and a plentiful harvest.

Donnacha Óg went ploughing for Lacken House and Eibhlín turned her hand to the potato-sowing. Everybody seemed to be out under the sky, out from the half-lit smoke and the damp floors and the verminous twitchings of the thatch. The children, still without school or master, banded together in the woods and in the low marshy places where they played a game that was new: redcoats and United men. Old folk sat alone before the doors, blinked and stirred from the drowsiness that lay on limb and in the blood as the sun spread full on mud walls and crinkled parchment skin.

On such a day, Donnacha Ruadh had the house to himself. Every time he walked across the threshold and took a few steps hither and thither with the light like a greyish yellow tinged veil on his eyes, he could have shouted out across the fields with pride in his newly found strength. All the spring days he had ever known were pressed together in his mind and their distilled power made him drunk. It was not one spring day but a thousand that possessed him: the air of all those days, not weary with ancient autumnal sunshine, but fresh, nourishing, pleasantly warm; water chattering to itself amongst stones and the ruck of gravel; the sky awesomely high, silken blue, with larks lost in it and streeling out songs; trees keenly green; children calling, crying, laughing, chanting broken, half-understood rhymes, and tired age defeated. The beggars and travellers would be taking to the roads, leaving cabins and ruins, barns and taverns, and the highways that swollen streams had made impassable would be open to horsemen, pedlars, carts, coaches, carriages, and all the wandering men and women of the tribes that can never stay still.

With his mouth quirked in a smile, Donnacha Ruadh scraped the warm clay reflectively with his stick. Was he not in excellent health? Hadn't he his strength back in full? By taking his time and by going cautiously, could he not go far?

He re-entered the house and fingering around the walls, found his good coat hanging in a corner. He took off his old coat and put on the other, pulling down the tails and lifting the collar around his neck till, as he thought, he was fitted out decently. Then from a pocket he produced a cravat which he knotted at his throat. He was ready. He laughed out aloud.

But he was all wary, his ears cocked for voices and footsteps, as he tapped his way along the track down from the house. The track seemed as steep as the roof of a mansion. He must be careful. He moved leisurely, halting to listen and to wonder how it was that in spite of his caution, heat prickled his skin and his lungs almost refused the mild, refreshing air. Still, he comforted himself, he was able to travel; he was travelling.

He heard a spade plugging into clay and scratching dully against rock. The digging stopped. He waited for the hail of a voice but it did not come, and then the digging was continued. In relief he blew out his breath lustily and went on downward, toeing and heeling the stony path, prodding before him right and left with the industrious stick.

He came to a place where another track fell across his own. There he raked about him hesitantly, tried one direction and found himself treading lush grass, tried the other way and stumbled against the butt of a wind-slanted hawthorn.

From his right a man called, 'Good day, master. Fresh and well you're looking. Are you taking a stroll? It's the day for it, anyway.'

He paused, meditating, thinking if he should answer, and softly cursing the speaker for being a loud-voiced boor. Mustering up heartiness, he replied, 'A fine day, thanks be to God. Aye, I'm taking a short stroll.' Then he smiled in admiration at his own cunning.

He walked left in desperation and prayed that he would hit the track that led to the road. For about twenty short nervous paces he swerved from side to side, from the grass to a stone wall and back again. Once stones rattled down, and to him their sound seemed thunderous. At last, he guided himself by the wall. The slope was steeper and his shoes slipped on greasy mould and weather-polished rock, but full of his success, he chuckled and whispered. If he could only reach the road, he might get a lift in a cart even for a little of the way, then another lift and another till in no time, maybe a week or a fortnight, he would be home.

Presently, when the warmth became heavier and there was not a stir in the sheltered air, he knew he was coming to the lowest path and the road. But the struggle had dazed and winded him, and his thumping heart importuned him for rest. But he would not halt yet. It was too dangerous amongst the neighbours working in the fields. He must get down where there were walls and high hedges to shield him from prying eyes.

The track was broad and level at last. Carts had rutted it and therefore it was near the road. He hastened.

But then, women began to call his name aloud and men shouted, seemingly from all sides, and suddenly, as the meaning of the cries possessed his mind, his strength fell from him like a coat and he was sick and cold.

'Master,' said the first man who reached him, 'what are you trying to do?'

Immediately, Eibhlín: 'Father, are you out of your mind?'

He lowered his head. 'Do you hear the children playing?' said he gravely, and spoke no more.

For they were all around him, men and women, badgering him angrily for frightening them with his tricks and for drawing them from their work. 'You'll go,' Eibhlín was saying. 'You'll go before the year is much older. After all I did for you, to think you'd make mischief like this! Shame on you.' They all said shame on him, but he did not lift his head or reply. And he was not sulking. He was smiling lightly and with a little twist of scorn on his lips.

They would send him home. They must. He had his way. They could not keep him now.

PART THREE

Last things

They have traduced and slandered Death.

(From the Irish.)

A man may see how this world goes with no eyes.
Look with thine ears: see how yon justice rails upon yon
simple thief. Hark, in thine ear: change places; and,
handy-dandy, which is the justice, which is the thief?

(King Lear.)

When I was marching o'er Wexford Hill,
Oh! who could blame me to cry my fill;
I looked behind and I looked before,
But my tender mother I ne'er saw more.

Farewell, father, and mother, too;
And sister Mary, I have none but you.
And for my brother he's all alone:
He's pointing pikes on the grinding stone.

(Traditional ballad.)

CHAPTER VII

The last journey

ı

At noon when they pulled up the cart at the foot of a long low hill running up between dusty hedges, they were overtaken by a party of horsemen.

It was Donnacha Ruadh, mumbling on a piece of hard oaten bread, who first heard the clattering at a great distance behind on the road. He bade his son cease hammering on the iron wheelrim that had come loose. Presently the son heard, too, and guided by his hearing, he lidded his eyes with cupped hands and peered across the shimmering fields. The glare dazzled. At last he perceived, rising in the sunlight like a mighty grey laborious smoke, the approaching cloud of dust. By then, the metallic hoofbeating was growing in his ears.

He wiped his forehead and let his arms fall limp to his sides. 'Now what's going to happen us?' he asked wearily. His father, sitting with his back to the mare, was mouthing the brittle bread unperturbed. The calmness irritated him. 'There's no fool like an old fool,' he added, his voice brisk. 'Didn't you hear enough during the past month to keep you safe in my house? You had even the priest telling you about martial law and proclamations and free quarters for the roving blackguards, and yet you...' He shut his two fists and, exasperatedly, flung them forward before him, open: 'Ah! Mother Mary.' The dust cloud was huge; the gallopade was hard.

'If you had brought me,' said Donnacha Ruadh levelly, 'if you had brought me, son, even before Easter when I asked you, you wouldn't be shivering now in your breeches with fright.'

The son sighed. 'There's no use in talk like that, father. All I'm afraid of is trouble and danger for yourself. You know it right well.'

'And all I'm sorry for leaving is your wife!'

The son walked out into the middle of the road. 'There,' said he. 'There you are. Red-coats, with carbines in their hands.' Quickly he added, 'I hope Máire and her household are safe. Free quarters! God in heaven, have mercy.' To his last grim words he heard the responding intake of breath and the feet-scuffle in the straw from the old man.

Then, the riders were about them, their mounts blowing and sweating. Resigned, his face set, the son leaned against the cart. The shaking, bobbing head of the officer's horse was within a yard of his face.

'Good day, good gentlemen,' said Donnacha Ruadh in English.

'Wait till you're spoken to. Here, you, stand from that wheel. Where are you going? What's your business? What's in this cart?'

The son stood.

The father heard the swish. He hiccupped with the upsurge of terror. The son, his neck and shoulder-blades smarting, swayed, and nervously licked the drops of perspiration from his upper lip.

'Good man, son. Good man.'

'More blasted rebels. Search this cart. Look under that straw. Empty the sack.'

The mare under the cart backed in fright and one of the soldiers dismounted and cuffed her right and left. Two of them, in rummaging the straw, heaved Donnacha Ruadh over, and he cried out as, his hat falling before him, his head struck against the tailboard. The shock stunned him. The son reached out to lift him upright. Between his spread shoulders he received a cut of a riding whip, then another, and yet again another. The whine of anger in the officer's voice reminded him, even as he winced, teeth searing gums in a clench, and back-muscles unloosed to the pain, of the crying of a dog protesting long before danger comes at all.

'Take the pair, and the cart. Here sergeant, you accompany them. Detail four men. Quite enough.'

Donnacha Óg gripped the cart-shaft with stiff straight arms and white-knuckled hands until, with straining against the impulse to shriek off the pain that burned in a slanting welt across his back, his ears sang and his mouth became dry, and wormy yellow lights burned before his shut eyes. Vaguely he heard the diminishing clatter of hoofs.

The air was quiet, warm and droning once more.

'All right, men. Take it easy.' It was the sergeant, hard-faced, English, brisk, yet strangely mild in his eyes. He held Donnacha Óg by the left arm to steady him. 'This,' said he, spitting, 'is a hangman's job. Egad, it's not soldiering.' Donnacha Óg started, but the man went on, cursing first with a rush of words such as neither the son nor father had ever heard. 'Get into this damned cart. Rebels? Why, they're making them as fast as a manufactory so as they can shoot 'em quicker. This morn he sees a child with a green ribbon and he goes at her. But I'm damned if he didn't strip off her ribbons and dress. Now I ask you! Children! Rebels! By God, he thinks he's Bonyparty.'

Donnacha Óg lay face downward on the floor of the cart and felt the skin on his back scorching itself to dryness, and took the grind and rock of the iron-shod wheels in his aching jaw-bones and shoulder joints. His father was sitting still, facing back towards the mounted, tired men behind, with countenance as calm, as immobile as a carving of whitish, old and very stained wood.

In a street-town of some two dozen houses, to the left of which stood a mansion among trees half-a-mile distant, the cart was pulled into a dung-smeared yard enclosed by an iron gate with lichened pillars. In sheds built against a wall were some of the horses of the party, and, in a corner, the musty, brittle remains of the previous year's hay. With his head reeling, Donnacha Óg stumbled over to the hay and lay down. His father stretched beside him.

Shadows were lengthening in the yard; the air was chilling off into twilit, refreshing coolness. Everywhere there hung the tang of burnt straw.

The father said: 'We've met hard blows and misfortune before this.'

'Are they gone?'

'They're gone, quartered on the village.'

'Quartered? How is it, will you tell me, father, that men, men, I say, endure the like of this without...' He choked with the revengeful constriction of his throat.

The horses were champing, hoofs scraping the cobbles. Out in the street no one seemed to be abroad, but yet the street was full of the resonant drawl of men's voices. No children at all were talking or laughing or even crying. The odours of many fires, wood-smoke and turf-smoke, of broiling meat and sizzling bacon and baking panbread, pervaded the evening like the promise of a feast, but stronger was the bitter smell of burning straw.

'Once, son, I thought it was holy patience that held us on the leash,' said the father, brightly and steadily. 'Now, in these days, at last I believe that it was not. I've seen many and many a generation coming and going from the womb to the grave, and they thinking on their passage that they alone were the best. I see now, now at the end of my days – and it's a thing I never wished to see – that we're falling, rotting, our strength departing, our passion, our desire to fight. The years when we fought belong to another world, of better men. And why do they, those English who have their will of us, why do they scourge us now? Surely they can't be afraid of poor belly-crawling mongrels? Son, I'm afraid that soon there will be no one of us all left in the land to mourn for the lost and the fallen and the virtue we once possessed. So be it.'

'You'll be gone from it before long.'

'Death? They slander death. But I'll go when I'm called. Will I ever get home?"

A low moon gained power as the day faded. The street was noisier then, with men gabbing and walking from house to house among their comrades. The two men in the shed caught the words of a bawled song that ended of a sudden with a curse, a scamper of booted feet and a dog howling.

> *Then merry be, my lads,*
> *And let us drink his health;*
> *We'll wish him honour and renown*
> *And what he wants of wealth.*
> *With a heigh down derry,*
> *Heigh down derry O-o-o-o.*

The iron gate was rattled and clanged. Donnacha Óg sat up with a start and gasped as his dried skin cracked rawly. The sergeant crossed the cobbles.

'Oh! you here still,' said he. 'Here, get out of this. You're safe. He's over at the mansion with a gutful of wine. He doesn't even remember you. He just waved his glass. But be careful. Be careful of your neck.' He jerked his head. 'There was some trouble here already; down the road.' He turned and strode away, leaving the gate wide open. They heard him barking out orders on his way down the street. He left a train of quietness behind him.

Donnacha Óg helped his father to mount the wheel, and taking the mare's head, he drew the cart out of the yard and walked before her down the street. There were lights, lamps and candles burning steadily, in many windows. On a few doorsteps and thresholds, soldiers were sitting and lounging with their red coats unbuttoned and their cravats unloosed. He walked stiffly, looking neither to right nor left for fear that from some doorway the command would come, the halt. His heart thumped as, unmolested, he came beneath trees that formed a sieve over-

114

head for the moonlight.

On the right where the moonlight poured down clear and strong, he saw smoke wavering lazily from a huddled mass that looked like a fallen rick. As he passed it, a woman glided barefoot across the road before him, and she naked to the waist, one breast and shoulder smeared black, and her hair down wild. Before his face, as he trudged, she waved her moon-whitened arms, and her mouth opened and shut soundlessly. She crossed the road twice, then turned, and padded back at a run in the dust towards the smoke uncoiling from a demolished house.

He stared ahead. He could not turn to look after her. Suddenly, he lost control of his rigidly held body, and raising his arm he lashed the mare, running with her as he did so, till the car was jolting and bouncing along, away from the village, the soldiers, the trailing smoke, the half-naked, crazed woman.

The father called: 'What is it, son? What's wrong?'

'Can you tell the living from the dead?' he shouted in reply.

II

Before they came through river mist, with cocks crowing, to the house on the other side of Kilmacthomas at all, the son knew what they were meeting in the eerie dawnlight. He was glad to God that his father, awake, nervously awake and alert like a sparrow, was stone blind.

Halfway up the street, he halted the mare to discover, with eyes hot for want of sleep, what the bulky shadows were in front of the houses. A fragment of a broken bottle tinkled before him. The noise made him muster his senses. He saw, ranged along the village, three unyoked wagons loaded with sacks, saddles, boxes and gear, and over by a gate, one gun, covered. Wisps of hay and straw littered the dust behind the wagons. In one place, where a bed of jet-black ashes stained the roadway, then greying under the early light, he distinguished stubs of charred, carpentered wood, pieces of furniture.

'Are we there?' asked Donnacha Ruadh. 'Are we passing through Kilmacthomas yet?'

'Easy! Speak low.'

'This is where I lived with your mother, lad. Do you remember? This is where I'd still be if I'd been a better man.'

'Whisper. Shut up. The soldiers are here, too.'

The son walked fast. 'They must have been mad here last night,' he murmured. 'There's not even a sentry. We're out of the houses now. Look. O Jesus Christ, shield us! Look!'

He dragged with all the pull of his weary muscles on the lumbering mare. Ahead to the left was the cartroad leading to the house of O Braonain, his sister's husband. He lifted his head to catch a glimpse of morning smoke or of the roof. Behind him he had seen more than he had ever expected at a great tree that now, in the tentative bustle and chirping of the new air, shook out a rush of whispering. There, from the lowest but yet high enough bough of the tree, with his head swathed in gagging blindfold rags, his clothes streeling in tatters that flittered with every fresh stir of the breeze, hung the limp, limb-pinioned body of a man at the end of a rope: swivelling almost imperceptibly, awfully, by the neck.

'What is it, son?'

The son would not answer. He swung the cart in on the softer clay of the lane, and it seemed that it was he who hauled the mare and cart, so desperate was his lunge up the narrow track.

The door of the house was shut. In the windows of the centre building with its slate roof, and in the windows of the thatched one-roomed additions at each side, there was only blackness. The windows were boarded from within.

The son pounded with his fists on the door.

Donnacha Ruadh was kneeling up, saying 'Ah-hah-hah!' in a breathless laugh.

Inside the house a chair was rattled. There was whispering. The shutter on one window was opened and shut, instantly, with a bang. Then the door swung open and a lean, grey-haired woman, thin-featured, aquiline, in the fifties like her brother who stood before her with upraised fists, put out her head timorously. She was wrapped in a man's surcoat.

She narrowed her eyes and shook her head.

'Máire, it's your brother. We're here. Your father. I bring your father home.'

'Máire,' said the old man, 'I'm home.'

She put her hands on each side of her head, against her ears, as if she were shutting out a bewildering thunder of voices, and with her hands thus, she said in a frightened hushed tone: 'Come in, come in. It's a queer house you come to. There's no man in the place, neither husband nor son, and there won't be till the militia go. They're hiding. Come in. O Donnacha, my brother, did they leave hands on you, too?'

The hearth was fireless and the rooms off the kitchen were as empty as a cave. But he was home.

After she had dressed, Máire fussed over them, over the old man especially, asking him what he would eat and drink to break his fast as though she had a fine larder in her keeping. She laughed lightly, apparently for nothing at all, but there was present in her gestures and her voice the calm, resigned weariness that women come to wear as a perpetual cloak after the business of loving and childbearing and housekeeping. The brother had slumped down in an elbow chair to doze and snore thickly, but the father was alert. He turned his head to follow the rapid movements of her feet, the blowing of her breath on the fire, the splash of milk, and the hollow scraping of a wooden pail across the flagged floor. He stamped his feet on the flags; they were good flags; it was a good house. Presently, after the heat of the new fire had soaked into his bones to draw sleep out, he smelled cakes baking on a griddle and his awakened hunger aroused him once more. The son slumbered. The day was coming in full, through the window at the back of the kitchen.

'Tell me, Máire, daughter,' asked the father drowsily, 'tell me how you look?'

She paused to look at him sharply. Then she laughed. 'Well, enough,' said she, 'with all the worry I have.'

'No, tell me, girl. Tell me the look of your face. Your voice is sprightly, and you laugh like a girl that'd be falling in love for the first time.'

'A girl! Go on out of that, father. I'm as grey as a badger. I have as many lines as yourself. In another ten years or less I'll be a hag with an edged face. Oh! father, surely you don't forget I'm old.'

'Aye,' he said. 'It's hard to keep from drifting back on the tide to the old times. Aye, we're not young any more.'

She sighed as a matter of course. 'Indeed we're not. My man, Seumas, is nearly as old as yourself.' She laughed lightly. 'He is, then. Himself and Seán are over in Boreen; and Brighid and Sighle are up there with another neighbour, too. They couldn't even get Mass last Sunday,' she added plaintively. 'Oh! it's dangerous for a man or a handsome girl. The North Corks are here, and they found a young lad, the fool, with an old musket and they hanged him, God protect us.'

Donnacha Ruadh started impatiently. 'Seumas?' he said, shrilly. 'Sighle? Seán? Who are they at all?'

She laughed again, this time hollowly, her gaze fixed on her father, for his erring memory shocked her. 'Why, father, Seumas is my man. Seán's the eldest. The other son's up in Tipperary. Sighle is the girl who got married last harvest and she's living up the lane about half a mile. And Brighid...'

'Donnacha,' said the old man, slapping the floor angrily with his stick. 'Wake up there, you bosthoon. Wake up and quit your yawning. There was a girl married out of this house last harvest, and I declare to God you never mentioned a word of it to me.'

'Aye,' said the son, yawning, 'and you sick and mad to come at the same time. We didn't want a funeral as well as a wedding in Knockanee.' He arose hurriedly. 'Don't be bothering me, anyway. I'm going out to the mare. I'm forgetting her.'

'The same odd pair,' Máire remarked, smiling. 'Always bickering.'

She gave the two men hot buttered griddle cakes, and hot milk with salt and pepper in it for seasoning. As they ate, wolfing the food, she bustled about the house, answering their questions, inquiring after her brother's wife, hardly pausing in her work to speak. It was only when her brother asked about the happenings in Kilmacthomas beyond that the hush came into her speech and her words became few.

'I was forgetting them,' said she, 'for the past hour, since you came. We go in fear in dark and day.'

She left the pair of them sitting there before the brightly dancing fire in its nook under the coping chimney-mouth while she went to milk the two cows and feed the fowl. A few chickens strayed into the kitchen, and clucked and picked across the floor in the track of sunlight from the window. The son, with his hands clasped in contentment on his paunch, savouring the good comfort and contrasting it, without envy or bitterness, with his own hillside home, surveyed the room drowsily, moved his gaze slowly from the smoke-blackened timber of the ceiling above the hearth, to the trapdoor of the loft, to the white cool walls, the plain stout chairs, the dresser, the shining dishes, and finally to the face of his father. The distress of the night's fantastic journey had exhausted all feeling in him, so that, dispassionately, he scrutinized his father's countenance and began to read in it what had featured it thus, so sparsely, so picked of flesh, so rutted and written with the tale of a lifetime and of all the people; and calmly, with no qualm of grief, he knew that this was the last time he would see that countenance moving in response to the soul within.

Above the thin straggling beard the mouth, sunken, lost its light smile as repose of sleep relaxed muscle and jaw; the nose, strongly arched, stood out from the narrow face; the eyes, beneath the high forehead, were shuttered with the pore-pricked shallow eyelids. From the crumpled body bundled in its clothes, the two legs protruded like barely fleshed bones set in shoes. All passion of the stronger kind was dried up in that frame and the most the body could do was to ache with hunger and thirst, fatigue, and the innumerable petty illnesses of its own break-up; even the memory of past passion was disappearing, leaving only those memories that, when the mind had been fresh in youth like newly trowelled clay, had been most deeply imprinted. Yet, there in the face, were the faint or bold vestiges of all printings or mouldings: youth that had to resign itself at last to poverty; the melancholy of frustrated effort, the regret of the spoiled priest; the restlessness that came from the depths of the soul; love of a woman; the imperious pride of the man of learning who believed himself to be set apart; and abiding anger against the plight of the whole people whose long term on earth had once been glorious and was now abject, a thing of the dust. Even the anger was gone; only the marks remained. But at least this shrivelled creature sinking there to a child's sleep had great and final comfort in knowing that all suffering on earth would soon end for him and that it would end amongst his own folk, with his daughter and her household, his grandchildren and, who could tell? his great-grandchildren; but he, the son, the tail of dying generations would remain only to see the end of everything. His daydream brought him repose. He shifted his chair closer to the fire till his feet rested on the hearthstone.

'We'll never have our own again,' he murmured in a bass monotone.

His father's eyelids twitched and blinked. So he too was asleep only in the body. The mouth spread in a gummy, pleasant, confident smile.

'You never know, son. You never know. God is not dead.'

With this phrase wreathing across his mind like an endless smoke, the son fell into a deep sleep.

I V

Donnacha Óg could not go home by the road he had come. It was too dangerous to approach the village. The hanged man had been cut down and buried, no one knew where, and it would be easy to swing another man in his place. So, Máire accompanied her brother northward towards boggy, reed-clumped fields and there set him on a cart track that, by a long round, would bring him homeward in the end. He said good-bye to his father casually, after his fashion, and muttered 'God is not dead.' Although neither son nor father hinted at it, each was sure that before they would ever look on one another again, one man would be dead. Since it was to be so, why grow sad?

It seemed to be no time after that when, one afternoon, a soldier, a dragoon with a shining helmet, galloped into Kilmac-thomas from Waterford, and soon the militia came running into formation in the street, rushing out of the houses they had made their own, readying the wagons and the gun for the road, curs-ing, snapping, ordering the womenfolk hither and thither. It was thus that the story was brought in the evening to Máire by a neighbour's child. 'They're going from our house,' said the child. 'They're called to Waterford. They're going.'

'Go down at once,' said Donnacha Ruadh, 'and see what you can. There's something mighty stirring.' He had brightened up sharply.

She hurried down the lane and inside a field, from the shelter of a hedge, she watched the march that was better news than unex-pected wealth to many a house. The hub-bub in the village had dwindled to quietness. A few stray dogs barked foolishly. Surly and silent the riders straggled by along the road with the sun at their backs and their shadows grasping before them gluttonously in the dust. In the same field and behind the same hedge but nearer the village, there were three women stooped to peer through the tangled bushes. Máire moved towards them. Together they watched through the dusty haze that settled in a grey film on the leaves and the roadside grass. One woman of the three, who crouched between her companions, counted the passing men in a dry whisper: 'Ten, eleven, twelve, thirteen, fourteen... Where is he? where is he?' Then, forgetting the count, she would begin it all over again, like an idiot winding up wool, dropping it, rewinding incessantly. She counted now as if every whisper of hers were an avenging musket-ball, or the neat plunge of a blade, or the voice of God crying the last and terrible words through her thin, trembling lips. The faces passed before her: dark, sullen, well-fed, well-drunken, chafing in every look even under the loose discipline of the march; and then the wagons went by, and in one of them, his battered face puffed and em-purpled, sat a swaying man, a labourer from some outlying farm with his hands bound behind him. The woman looked at him keenly, shook her head and ceased the counting. 'He's not mine,' said she. Distantly, the clipclop of the hooves and the squeaking and rumble of the wheels dissolved into the afternoon. Floating dust subsided. And into the village, like prisoners released suddenly, the women and the children and a few old men, most of them old, gathered hilariously. Soon, the men and the boys came pouring in from all sides, over walls, over hedges, down from the cabins and barns and lofts where they had been in hiding.

Máire went amongst the people. She found herself as hysterical as the rest, repeating what she had heard, answering her own questions, raising her voice into frenzied shouting, kissing men and boys who had not dared walk abroad in daylight. She would have news for her father that would drive all his years back in retreat.

The men were shouting.

'They'll get what they've earned.'

'There'll not be one of them left alive.'

'Is it true there's fighting east of Waterford?'

'They hanged a good man, by God.'

'There's fighting.'

'They burnt my house.'

'There's fighting in Wexford.'

'The priests are leading the people.'

'Chapels were burned.'

'They destroyed God's house.'

'Is it true, O is it true that the men are fighting?'

'They've taken towns.'

'It's true.'

'The English are running.'

'There's a battle all over Ireland.'

'Why aren't we fighting?'

'The priests are the leaders.'

'A man told me. He swears it.'

And so it went on like a running fire, bursting into flame here, lowering there, rising again. The crowd broke into groups. All were talking together. The groups mingled and separated, driven like leaves in the erratic scurries that presage a mighty storm, a storm that will upturn all things. They gestured. They babbled. They ran from group to group. They beat their hands together. The storm was seizing their souls.

Máire walked across the fields to her own house. Her father was shuffling up and down the kitchen. When she told him what she had seen and heard he passed the palm of his right hand

121

across his face, and for a second she fancied that his dead eyes had kindled fire.

'No,' he said. 'No, no, no. God is not dead.'

V

Immediately, or thus it appeared to Donnacha Ruadh, the house was packed with people. They swept him to his elbow-chair. Bewildered, the news of the fighting rumbling in his mind, he could say only 'Ah! Ah! as they shook his hands and clapped his shoulders. Máire was protesting that they would kill him. He heard her husband, Seumas, praising him for his vigour and his great years, and welcoming him home, and all he could do by way to reply was to nod his head and to move his hands up and down from his knees. Seán, the grandson, spoke shyly and pressed his hand manfully. The two granddaughters, Brighid, and Sighle the married one, and her husband Piaras O h-Aiceid, greeted him with hints at the stories they had heard of his adventures, his sayings, his verse-making and his schoolmastering. He turned on them suddenly: 'Don't keep me waiting long for great-grandchildren. They'll be no good unless they see me.'

'I'll do my best,' said Piaras.

'Let the two of you do your best,' said he.

They laughed. The wildness of the laugh hurt him. He detected how near it was to weeping. For evil had departed and with the relief, they were crazed.

He tried to add to their joy. Seumas the son-in-law, a man nearing his sixtieth year, had grown, he said, into a fine young fellow; and Brighid, he was sure, already had the eyes of the boys of the parish on her. Sighle, he declared, wouldn't know where she was or what had happened to her before she'd have a houseful. And if Seán, the grandson, didn't speak up for himself soon, he'd find a fine strapping girl running away with him under her arm. He mumbled on, trying to remember the names and the sound of their voices, and soon, as their attention and talk were withdrawn from him, he recognised that they were tiring of his chatter.

He listened, laughing when they laughed, nodding when one of them spoke. He began to distinguish one voice from another, the slide and thump of boots from the clapping of shoes on the flag-stones, the tone of a cough, the fall of a single word. Máire's voice he could pick out of a tumult: it had the coolness, the calm flow at times, that belonged to her mother. Brighid, he noted, was determined, firm-footed, self-assured, a girl who would fashion a household to her own liking. Sighle, he decided, was a bit light-headed, but yet as warm-hearted as any man could wish. Her husband, Piaras, he could not account for at all: the man seemed to be nowhere, a dim spare-worded figure on the edge of the crowd. Seumas, his son-in-law, he knew of old as a quiet man, cumbersome of speech but slow and sure as the advance of a plough. And Seán, the grandson, he was of his own nature in ways, sharp-tongued when he spoke at all, but now dim among all the voices like the other man, Piaras. The voices were all going together, and as he listened, he could not tell which was which but only that the people were glad and that he, sitting there before the fire, was unheeded.

They were paying him no heed. He did not care a brass farthing. It was as he had wished, and their incoherent gabble was a blessing on his head. He was amongst his own, set down in the last house he would dwell in after all his wandering, so settled already amongst them as to be unnoticed like the familiar well-used chair, like the hearthstone itself before which a mother and father had aged and children grown and sorrow had been endured and joy taken. A road ribboned out endlessly in his mind over hills and along valleys and across treeless bogs, through villages and the tortuous streets of the towns, and he smiled as he thought that he would never have to travel such a road again for ever and ever. Nor, thinking thus, did he turn his mind towards what yet lay before him: the last ford to cross, the last pass. The warm, companionable, singsong of voices held him to the place where he sat. He searched his memory for the high phrases – which he was sure he once knew – that had been uttered by salt-stained, storm-hardened Odysseus beaching his ship for the last time on the friendly coast of his forefathers; but nothing rewarded his searching except the quietly muttered words, 'I've beaten the sea. I'm home.'

CHAPTER VIII

The last fight

I

During all those summer days, passing with the speed and dimness of a dream, the news from which he had at first withheld the complete trust of his mind, came to the village continually, assuring him beyond all doubt that somewhere in the east the people had arisen in red, fiery war.

Exaltation mingled with terror, such as he had not experienced since he first went through danger on the sea, abode with him wherever he was.

Men, unafraid, were out with weapons in their hands after the death-sleep of generations. That was what he wanted to hear. They could tell him that soldiers were moving through every parish and that mail-coaches were not running, and that ships at Waterford carried families flying from the wrath of men who had been scorned, but what were such stories?

'I thought that the last and the best of us were dead in the grave,' was the refrain of his most urgent speech. 'Either the dead have arisen or the living have been gifted with new life. God prosper them.'

Seumas O Braonain, Máire his own daughter, all of them tried to twist his thoughts towards other things, but inevitably his mind would return; and when they warned him that the priests had already spoken against the rebels, he said 'Bah!' as to the priests: 'Bring me Father O'Brien. Bring me that young curate. I'll tell him.'

They brought the curate to the house one evening, a young, lively, fairhaired man who preached Sunday after Sunday against violence but who had dared to walk up the village street, as protection for a girl, when the militia had been making their own of the place.

'Ha! ha! so you were preaching again, Father,' said Donnacha Ruadh. 'Well, preach and preach. All Wexford is up and words will not stop them. They've run the English out of Enniscorthy, Father, and they're storming New Ross and they'll take Waterford yet, and Dublin itself with all its mansions and fine people. Preach and preach...'

'But, friend...' the priest would begin.

'I know. I know. You were in France, in your college when all the old ways were overturned and the king and queen killed and men murdered by mobs. You have a hatred of blood-spilling. Preach and preach. Aye, you'll be listened to and heeded, but it would be better for you to hold your tongue and to...

'With all honour to your coat, Father, you haven't seen what I have seen. Now the day is in our hands. Oh! I wish I were a young lad. I wish I could meet a man of them. I wish I could shake his hand...

'Did you ever see a mongrel dog, Father O'Brien, scuttling away from his own shadow? Did you ever see a quiet harmless timid man being insulted and beaten and then he turning with his fists shut and his manhood in his eyes? I tell you there's no use in talking about the people and their Faith if you don't heed them now. That's all they have, the Faith, but do you think, Father, they could hold on to it for ever if they were to be denied everything else through injustice till the day of doom? Do you...'

They would allow him to exhaust himself and then, in their even, unruffled conversation, pretend that he had not spoken at all over there by the fire, had not raised his voice till it shrilled and broke. Listening afterwards to them he fancied that he heard them through the clouds of a dream to which they belonged and that he was sleeping an endless sleep in another place and during another time. The clouds were growing about him. Or was it weariness that was weighing down his eyelids and making the hearing indifferent and the head loll heavy on the neck? They were leaving him alone as they would leave an annoying child who presently will fall into a doze. Let them do as they pleased. He had his litany, an increasing litany of names from the fighting that could be repeated one after the other as battle-cries running along a line of advancing men: Oulart, Enniscorthy, New Ross, Wexford, Gorey, Newtownbarry, Oulart, New Ross, Enniscorthy, Wexford, Gorey... sustaining exaltation even when sleep truly came down as easily and as graciously as the wide, heart-healing night.

I I

Like muttering from sleepers, news came out of the east: battles, towns taken and lost, villages burned to the ground, men hanged, shot, beaten to death: fragments of stories that could not be pieced together into a single tale.

The corn turned in the fields; apples hung on the heavy boughs in the mansion orchards where moss was flossy and high walls lichened green with great age; the work of the fields went on, and soon the stubble would be bare to a mellowing sun or the broad, yellow moon.

'Maybe they'll be our own fields some day,' said Donnacha Ruadh, 'when the men will come out of the east.'

III

He lay awake one night on his bed over in the corner to the left of the hearth. Autumn, he recognised by the chill, was already in the nights, in the low-rising mists and the bleak, deserted stubble fields. With a lethargic west wind his thoughts were going as he lay, following its track across the heaving wheat and oats that stood uncut, heeding its secretive disputation in doomed glenwoods, its lost crying in old houses with gapped roofs and swinging shutters and open cupboards – houses where, as a wanderer, he had slept – fancying how it foraged insistently through orchards till overripe unplucked fruit plumped down into thick rank grass, like the tired, sated childless men of rich and lordly lineage dropping into glutted family tombs: following that west wind over all Ireland to the country by the eastern sea where men had fought. In houses farther up the laneway, dogs were barking angrily. In the house around him, so warm and shielding, all were asleep. By and by he heard a crunching of the gravelled dust in the lane, the snapping of a dry twig and then a scratching of a dog's paws on the wood of the door. One of the womenfolk, turning in her sleep, sighed and moaned faintly. It is a dog, he thought, but a tapping, timid as of fingertips, brought him to his feet on the cold flagstones. The lethargic west wind enveloped the house once more with its soft hissing and passed by; and he lifted his head as if he saw its passage.

He waited. The tapping began again, louder this time. He put out his hands and groped his way to the door. He put his ear to the jamb. The tiny draught whistled against his eardrum, chill and piercing. There was a stirring in the dust outside the door. Lifting the wooden bar from its iron crook, he pulled back the leaf a few inches, saying,

'Who's there?'

'Let me in.'

It was a man's whisper.

'Who are you?'

'Let me in, in the name of God.'

Donnacha Ruadh swung the door open slowly and reaching out suddenly, brushed a face that was hot, wet with perspiration and prickly with an unshaven beard. 'Come in softly,' said he, 'or you'll wake the house.'

He led the man across to the bed that stretched low on the edge of the subdued red fireglow, and pushed him gently down so as to be seated. The man shrank of a sudden.

'Are you hurt some place?' asked Donnacha Ruadh. 'Are you?'

'Are you friends?'

'Wait till I call the woman of the house.'

The man grabbed at him out of the darkness. 'Are you friends, tell me?'

'Who are you? How do I know?'

'Hush! Answer me.'

'You're in an honest house. Will that do you?' said Donnacha, and going across the kitchen, he called out his daughter's name, and as he did so he heard the man saying, 'Oh! but I'm spent and worn.'

Donnacha felt his way back by the wall and got in under the bedclothes behind the seated man who was tensely alert then, listening.

Máire lit a tallow candle.

'What is it, father?' she asked, and paused.

Seumas had come down too and then Seán. The old man could hear the pad of their bare feet across the floor towards the bed, then the halt, and he guessed that they were standing the up-lifted candle. The stranger was pressing hard on the edge of the bed with his two hands behind him, strained for the upleap.

'Máire, get him a bite at once. He's hungry.'

'You're hurt, sir,' said she. 'There's blood on your shirt.'

'Yes,' said the man. 'It's nothing, a snick of a cut. I lost my coat.'

'You're young. Your voice is young,' Donnacha Ruadh said instantly.

Then Seumas spoke, slowly and quietly. 'You're young to be in the fighting, to be out with the rebels?'

The man was up, stepping away from the bed towards the door, stepping around by the walls as if he were working his way to escape.

Curtly, the old man said, 'We're friends. Sit down.'

'I'll take someone's life if one of you...'

'Didn't I tell you we're friends? Máire, get him a meal this instant. Seumas, take a look at that scratch of his. And Seán, go get him a coat. Man, you're as safe as the men across the seas. This is an honest house – it is, as long as I'm here.'

IV

Safe he remained during the four days he rested with them, and the wound in his right forearm, the graze of a musket-ball, healed fast. They took his clothes from him and fitted him out, despite his protests, in the Sunday suit that belonged to Seán. Even so, their kindness could not melt the icy secrecy that bound him; and he was almost as strange to them as on the night he slipped in the door. While there was a stem of daylight in the sky he did not stir abroad at all, and only when it was dark would he walk for an hour or two with Seumas or with Seán. 'We can't tell our friends from our enemies,' said he. 'We don't know what hand is against us.' He walked fearfully, responding jumpily to the murmurs and bickering of the night, warily watching shadows, trees, ricks, houses. By night he slept on the floor before the fire in the kitchen. He slept thinly. Of many an hour of that thin, disconnected sleep Donnacha Ruadh could tell. The man would doze for a while, then lift and turn irritably, with teeth grinding, and suddenly cry himself wide awake for an hour or two of furtive movement and of barefooted pacing up and down the flagstones and of listening beside the door or the window.

On the last night of his stay he was pacing like that when, of a sudden, he said in English, 'I wonder where they are?'

'Who?' said Donnacha Ruadh softly.

'What's that?'

'Go on. Talk, or you'll be a lunatic with strain.'

'There were three of us; three of us on the run for our lives.'

'I suppose they're as safe as you are. Where did you leave them?'

The man sat down and said eagerly, 'We scattered after getting through Waterford, sneaking along the streets. I was ready to lie down, I was that spent. They dragged me on.'

'They were good men.'

'I suppose it'll be many a year before I set a foot in Wexford again, if our house is left standing at all.'

He poked with a stick at the embers and added a piece of bogwood that shortly began to fume, and to crackle faintly like distant musketry fire.

128

'What's your name, lad?'

'I said it doesn't matter. It doesn't. Do you hear that? Their guns were as thick as that crackling. My name doesn't matter. We were beaten. We were down from the start. Nobody stirred to help us. Worth it, was it? So your folk said. That's salt on a useless wound,' said he vehemently.

Donnacha waited. He knew other words would follow, because for the first time as he perceived, the suspicion which kept the young man tongue-tied was vanishing, and a new anger, nourished by regrets and the ruin of a defeat, was smoking up into flame.

V

'I went into it,' said the man, reflectively, 'like a straw being whisked into a torrent in a shower.

'Now, I don't know where I am. Why did it all happen? I took a chance with my life when I came into this house but there's many another house where they'd hold me for the hangman.

'What's wrong at all? I went into it, fully sure that every man in Ireland was... But now the priests are against us, and priests led us; now the people are against us, and who were we but farmers and labourers and tradesmen like anyone else? I have nothing now.' He jabbed at the fire. Little flames were flapping. 'I was to be married this autumn.'

He crouched, silent, for a few minutes, staring at the flourish of flag-like flames and listening to the sputter of the burning wood, while his mind called up the agony of the days through which he had lived mad.

'The last time I saw her,' he continued, 'she was in her own house.

'Now, why isn't she there still? Why am I here and not in my own country? Why...'

He flung the stick from him into the fire so that, for an instant, the flames cowered.

'I was coming in from my work – the potatoes' – said he, calmly, 'when I dropped in for a word. I lived with my mother and a sister. I have two brothers; one is with a gentleman in Dublin and the other is across the sea, in England, soldiering for all I know.'

He lowered his voice to an almost inaudible murmur.

'I tell you I was drawn into it like a straw into a runnel. Other men went into it with their eyes open and their minds made up. But I was no United man. I was never sworn in. You see, I couldn't be, because the gentleman my brother worked for was a government man and I couldn't be a party to treason...

'But you couldn't be a Christian and not go when you were called to go,' he began with the steady flow of speech that, except for brief brooding pauses, continued till morning lit the window and mocked the lingering smoulder of the fire. 'I'll remember what I saw and what I heard of the soldiers and the yeomen and the militia. There was nothing of evil they didn't do to the people, nothing on God's earth. They lived and lodged with us – not in my house because it was too far from the outer billets – and for thanks and payment they gave us the boot and the carbine-butt. When anyone opened his mouth to protest or to complain to a magistrate, the house went up in red flames and smoke. I recall one night I was out trapping rabbits. That night I saw the whole of the sky in the north as fiery as if the sun had gone down: thatch, hayricks, everything. And then the women and the girls weren't safe even behind locked doors. There was one young lad taken near our place and hanged after they had used a pocket knife and... another man, the father of a family who was found with a prayerbook in his pocket, he was tied to a pump and a patch of calico full of boiling steaming pitch was slapped down on his head and then torn off. They bared him to the skull-bone. Did you ever hear a horse screaming in your life? That was it. Neighbours found the man, down by the stream. He was alive all right but he was past all sorrowing for he didn't recognise his own children nor his wife nor the land he walked and worked.

'Faith, you might well say it, there was many a man dead with the drouth for revenge. I know I was. I was no United man, though. I wasn't looking for fighting of set purpose. I had never been sworn in. The priests kept the rein on us. Father Michael was our priest, and says I to him one evening on the road after he had given the Last Sacraments to a flogged man flung in a field, "Father," says I, "you preached last Sunday all about loyalty to the government and the king and I wondered if it was holy patience you had or a stone for a heart!" He just looked at me and says he, "Even stone will break."

'Then they called for me, neighbours that I know like the palm of my hand, honest hard-working folk who never wanted anything but to keep a roof over their heads and to rear up children well and to find good husbands for their girls. Peter Foskin was the spokesman. He was a sworn one, sure enough. He had a fowling piece in his hand and he gripped it bravely. The other men in our yard had pikes and billhooks and an old gun between them. "Well," says Peter Foskin, "are you with us? We're fighting." I didn't know what to say. "Look," says Peter, pointing east. I looked. Where the chapel was, smoke rose red, "Where's Father Michael?" I asked, playing for time. Peter smiled at me and says, "Out rousing the parish." My mother was standing behind me at that minute and when I turned to her she said, real gently, "Go on, son." And so I crossed the yard with them and picked a pitchfork from the wall. "That," says Peter, "will do you well enough until you win better." By God he was a good man. He kept the heart in every one of us, shivering as we were in our shoes.'

The fire had finished its sprightly, noisy burning and was settling down to a quiet glow. Donnacha Ruadh waited for the voice.

'Peter lined us up in a little grove that's on the other side of the hill from the road, and he bade us lift our heads and not to be shambling along like grumbling harvesters. He told us that we'd be meeting trouble before dark on the other side of the hill because, says he, "The yeomen will be coming back and they'll get paid by Father Michael if all goes well and if ye're men." He sent a man up the heather, and another one down to the road and another one to the end of the grove. We sat down then. It was a warm evening but we – I was anyway – we were as cold as marble. I don't know how many times we went to drink. There wasn't a man of us who wasn't glad when Peter said, "Up now." The signal had been given. But there wasn't any fire in us and so Peter began to urge us, saying, "Come on, boys. Do as I tell you."

'Up the hill we went and soon there was no need for urging. There was a rattle of carbines from the other side of the hill. "That'll be the yeomen," says Peter. There was a blast of a hunting-horn. Then Peter shouted, "That'll be Father Michael. Come on, men. Down with you now like the hammers of hell."

'We had time only for a bare look from the brow of the hill, just a flash like you'd get from a falling shutter, and then we were running. There was yeomen on the road on rearing horses, and they were slashing with swords at the men all around them and letting off guns. Miles away, I saw fires. We went down to the horsemen like a pack of hounds in full cry, every man shouting. Oh! but we came down like the rockfall in a quarry. We were over the wall with a tumble of stones and in the middle of it, and as sure as I'm sitting here, Peter Foskin leapt it and began swinging his gun by the barrel. I was on the wall with the fork in my hand when a yeoman came at me and I jumped with the fork stiff before me. He went down. All I can recall after that is darting here and there, dodging hoofs and the cleaving swords, and lifting up men by the boots from the saddles. Then what was left of them ran. They cleared.

'It was Peter who called us back from the chase, bawling at us like a demon and calling us fools. We came back. There was Father Michael on his own black mare, with belts on him in proper style and a sword in his hand. And there was a flag, a black one with a bit of green on it, the best they could get at the time. Most of the men were strangers or half-strangers to me. There was a young lad with a drum. There were guns too, and pikes aplenty. That was our start.

' "Well, Father," says Peter proudly, "we worked that one all right."

'Father smiled sourly. "Not so much howling the next time, Peter. Forewarned is forearmed. Ye frightened them off. Now men, get into ranks of four. Quick there. You and you, see to those three wounded there. We're off to do real hard work."

'If I were to tell you all we did in the next few weeks, I'd be here for as long again, talking without a stop. But the time didn't seem like a few weeks. They were like hundreds of years of marching and running and dodging with your clothes on night and day and your belly growling with the hunger and your face blackened with powder and dirt and fire. When I think of it now, the clearest thing I remember is not the killing nor the danger but the dragging walk along the roads.

'Anyway, the night after our first fight, our numbers grew. We spent the time around a fire, a big bonfire that raised our hearts, while men came sidling up the hill from all the quarters, men with pikes and guns and flags, some of them singing, and some of them boasting of what they had done that day. For the first time I believed that all Ireland was up and armed and singing...

'Don't ask me how long after that it was when the next fight happened. There was a house, a mansion in a district I'm not familiar with. The men had spoken of it. A baronet owned it, a dog of a man, they said, who had raised the worst and most savage yeomen of the place. Months before he had persuaded all the farmers, on the promise of leaving them all in peace, to take an oath that they'd be loyal to the King. They had given up every weapon too, even fowling pieces and old guns that hadn't smelt powder in a generation. He was a dog. Because then, when all that was done, he let the soldiers and the yeomen do as

132

they pleased. Well, we came to the mansion from all sides. Doors were barred and the windows shuttered. The first of us got a welcome and two of our best were laid low. Father Michael being gone towards the east, towards the sea, Peter Foskin was our captain. He sent a message up to the house, asking if there were any women in it and that if there were, they could go safely with a conducting party. There were no women. "All the old women in Wexford are around the house, playing at soldiers," was the return message. We attacked then. Under the shelter of the fine front porch with its tall pillars, we dragged a stump of a tree up to the door and after battering like mad, we broke in. There wasn't much fight after that. The flames did the burying.

'We moved west because, as we were led to believe, we must strike up with men from other counties. And there was a village and another fight. That was a big fight, the biggest, and the last I was in. By that time I was beginning to forget altogether I ever had feet or that I ever ate beside my own fire or slept in the comfort of my own bed.

'The houses of this village – it was only one street – were packed with soldiers. We were about five hundred then and we spread out across the fields one morning, just with the first light, and crept closer behind the walls and hedges. We had keen scouts but they were not quick enough for all the sentries and so, by the time we swept in, marching like good soldiers with the musket-men in front to blast a road for the charge of the pikemen, the village was ready. "They have a gun, I'm told," Peter Foskin said. "Maybe we'll borrow it afterwards. It would be mighty useful." But that wasn't to be. By the time we came within a few hundred paces of the houses, the yeomen and the soldiers had drawn up behind the walls. "Don't fire," says Peter, "till you're sure of your man." Then he said, "I wish Father Michael were here." It was the first and last word of defeat he uttered.

'The whistle went and the shout was raised and we made our rush. The musket-men halted and some of them knelt down for steady aim. They fired as soon as the soldiers fired. I was behind in the long line with the pikemen, and you could hear the balls hissing and droning by your ears. A few men fell near me. Then we were off on our charge, with the pikes low and ready. But before we reached the soldiers at all, the bugle went, and they fell back in order, odd men stopping to fire. They ran back into the street, into the houses for shelter, and began firing from the windows and the doors. We tried to come as near as we could, and where we were shielded we knocked holes in the walls of the houses or flung lighting sticks up on the thatch. We stabbed in through windows and doorways, and the place was thick with dust and clouds of smoke, and everybody was shouting so that the din must have been heard miles away. It must. For that would account for what happened when the soldiers took to their heels, on foot or on horses; that is, any of them we didn't catch.

'Like fools we followed down the road after them, running when we should have been attending our wounded and dressing our ranks and sending out scouts and messengers. Below the village the road swung round a clump of trees to a bridge with a high single arch. We swept around, with Peter Foskin in our midst and he screaming at us to halt and return. He was right. We were fools.

'The red-coats were there before us. There they were with a gun set, and the gunner beside her, ready to give her the spark. They had been waiting for us. The gunner was waiting for us. Down whent his hand – I saw it – down went his hand when we were all jumbled together, tearing at one another to get to shelter, losing our long pikes and falling. It was like short vicious thunder. Then a gap was cut, a gap of smashed and broken men, and the dust was puddled with blood. The soldiers fired their carbines, and the horsemen charged out from the fields.

'I fell over Peter Foskin. I knew he was dead. His head was slashed. I crawled free and made for a clump of bushes and running low I got through them down to the stream and across it and up the fields behind the hedges. I ran and ran, and fell and crawled until fear was gone. All of a sudden I remarked how quiet everything was, how the birds were singing to themselves, and how hot was the blaze of the sun. Not caring about anything I rolled into a dry ditch, full of ferns, and slept. There was never sleep like it. It was the awakening that made me...

'Aye, that was it. That was defeat. I was sure of it. We had been slaughtered before the bridge. I was sure of it. How was I to know that the fighting would go on in other places and that towns had been taken and battles won – and lost. That was defeat.'

He sighed and stretched his legs, and then, looking around him, said, 'The morn's here.'

Sleepless, Donnacha Ruadh muttered. 'And the rest? What happened then?'

The young man laughed in mockery. 'Oh! the rest, is it? I met

134

with two other men, running, too, in fear. I don't know how we ate or slept or which day I got this gash in the arm. That's all the living have out of it all: scars and wounds and crippled limbs. The dead men won't care. That was defeat.

'We crept like beaten dogs through the villages and past the houses. In some places, where they fed us and gave us an out-house for sleeping, we heard news, gone on before us, of the fighting. The fighting seemed to be years old, like a far-away bad dream, and there was some pleasure and a great peace in walking across the country by night with nothing to trouble us save the dogs. There was one day – the last before we crossed the river in a fishing-cot that nearly drowned us – when we stretched on our backs on a hill. Shooting began below. We found where it came from. Soldiers, like little red insects, were riding in a line across a wide yellow cornfield, birds rising before them, but it wasn't birds they were after. We saw men starting up from the corn, holding up their hands for mercy as the soldiers closed around, and all that was left behind was a trampled dark patch. That was defeat.'

'Defeat!' said Donnacha Ruadh. The young man was finally silent. 'Defeat!' he repeated, and shook his head. 'Who knows? You haven't seen the generations passing, dead. You fought.'

The young man yawned and kicked at the sparks that remained on the hearth.

V I

When the dark came around again, he went. He took the bundle they gave him, a shirt, stockings and some oaten bread, and very solemnly but quite silently the while, he shook hands with them.

'Will you not stay?' asked Donnacha Ruadh. 'You're safe here.'

He stood for a second, shifting his feet. 'I... I...' he began and smiled regretfully.

'He knows his own business,' said Máire. 'He came unhin-dered.'

'Let him go like that,' added Seumas.

'I don't mean that,' said the young man. 'I mean I'll not be easy ever while... O, I'll go. Good-bye to you all, and God be with you.'

Seumas and the son went with him.

Máire fussed about the house and whispered to Brighid while Donnacha remained near the door, following the footsteps that

CHAPTER IX

The last twilight

I

When you become not so much old as very aged by the ceaseless weathering that men endure between the womb and the clay, you hardly notice, no more than a child, how the days pass and how, between sleep and sleep there is only a shadowy sway of the light like the pendulum swing of a dying lantern swinging in ever diminishing curves in a corner to final, unlit, unalterable stillness.

Desire, wanting, wishing, subsided. Grass withering before frost into the protective clay. Once more he sank among the roots, the close, matted, warm memories out of which he had sprung.

In his inner world, voices at first strange murmured amiably and faces at first unfamiliar glimmered and became clear as the face of his mother and the sharp commanding countenance of his father: folk whom he could not have summoned up in memory once upon a time, try as he would. Uncalled, they came.

'I once fished for salmon in the Shannon with my bold Tom Lillis. Tom was a man and a half. A sailor. He saw the Indies and Africa and... Maybe Tom could tell me now...'

'The day my father sent me to school with my first pair of new breeches, there was no master. He took Horace too much to heart the wrong way, the poor man. Drunk.'

'Will you tell my father I'm not...'

He would check himself, recognising that his wits were wandering, and thus save himself from uttering complete folly about returning ghosts.

'So you think I'm going foolish with age, do you?' he would say to whoever was near.

Besides, the recurrent complaining of his failing flesh forbade him to stay among his phantoms. The pitiable flesh felt every chill, shivered and protested, and in spite of himself he groused, pushing away the food, twisting restlessly on his bed, dozing and gnawing with toothless gums in reply to the cruel, ineluctable invitation of the grave.

Máire, her husband and their daughter let him be and watched him without anxiety, for what was coming was to come. Pityingly, but yet resigned they watched him in the morning when, especially with mist lying on the fields, he coughed and wheezed dryly and choked with a horrible retching, sucking of breath. On Sundays he prayed at home now, and about once a fortnight the priest came to see him. On sunny days they brought him out before the wall and set him in his elbow-chair with a great coat on his shoulders. He would not allow them to carry him. 'What do you think I am? A child or a cripple? You insult me.' Walking that short distance across the kitchen floor seemed infinitely laborious and painful for him, a movement made foot by foot, his head bobbing, his fist clutching his stick and trembling. Once he was out under the sun he became calm, drowsy with tales that never moved straight and never ended. He would sit and tell them to himself, alone there beneath the eaves where the swallows nested and chittered and flipped and watched clay returning to clay.

II

Máire, to shake him out of the increasing lethargy, brought him a young scholar, a neighbour's son who, in that autumn, would go to the new college in the midlands to be a priest.

'Yes! That's where I'm going,' said the scholar. He listened patiently to the dragging, long premeditated phrases of the old poet.

'No, you're wrong, child. Abroad. You're going abroad. France.'

'I beg your pardon.'

'Italy, maybe. No priests can get... no college here. No, child. We always went abroad.'

'Times change, sir. You must know that...'

'I must not. You speak the English well, lad. Like a gentleman – if it's a compliment. Times change. The English, aye!'

'You were... I mean, you are a notable scholar, sir.'

'Latin, now. You must have your Latin. Aye, they couldn't puzzle me. Try me.'

The scholar laughed.

'Try me with the king of them. Virgil, child!'

'All right, sir. You begin where I leave off.'

'Go on, go on, go on.'

'Aeneas is descending amongst the dead to find his father, and

Virgil is seeking power of speech from the gods to describe the journey.'

'Good. Good, lad.' The white beard bobbed in commendation, the mouth yawned, and the crusty tongue hung loose within as he chuckled.

'*Di*,' began the scholar, '*Di, quibus imperium est animarum, umbraeque silentes*... now, sir.'

'Wait a minute, child.' He fingered the coat around his shoulders and listened for a moment to the swallows' twitter above his head; then, slowly, breathing heavily, he spoke: '*Di, quibus imperium est animarum, umbraeque silentes, et Chaos, et Phlegethon, loca nocte tacentia late...*' And thus he went on with the invocation to the gods to whom belongs the governance of souls, to the inaudible dead and Chaos and Phlegethon, places where silence hems the night around. His eyes were screwed up as he searched the roads and profound tracks of his memory that were as dark as the ways that Aeneas discovered bravely. '*Ibant obscuri sola sub nocte per umbram,*' he repeated, '*perque domos Ditis vacuas et inania regna.*' Instantly he turned it into Irish, saying, 'They moved invisible through shadows in the lonesome night, through the empty halls and forlorn realm of Dis... That's from the master of all masters. Do that, you, Mr. Scholar, with your gentleman's English.' Then he swung back again to the Latin, to the same lines that he mumbled as intensely and as tenderly as a man would murmur the bywords between himself and his woman. He strove to move from them, to continue, but they bound him, and all he could get into his memory were images of leprously lit darkness and gibbering obscene and filthy creatures, and a great broad river rushing heedlessly on into the engulfing night. Where was the boatman, Charon? What were the lines about his goatish hair and flaming eyes? O, what were they? He bent his head and knocked against his forehead with his fist knobbled with bone, and said, 'Nobody at home. Nobody at home.'

'*Huc omnis turba ad ripas effusa ruebat,*' the scholar complacently.

That was it. Hushed, he muttered to himself. The dead hosted to the shore, men and women full of years, heroes, young maids and youths destroyed in their prime. They came like leaves clipped by the first frosts of autumn, shoaled along in a wind; like birds flocking to the sunny lands across the empty seas, away from the winter gales and the cold. But what were the lines? *Huc omnis turba.* He rubbed his forehead feverishly with his hand to banish the nightfall of his mind. Yet, in this agonising nightfall a music beat out majestically such as had beaten in his mind when, his faculties alert, he had often recited to himself on long journeys afoot or in his school in the mountains the lines fashioned by the Roman. The old Roman, wasn't he, too, gone amongst the dead, gliding soundlessly as all men in the midst of thin ghosts where pain, broken honour, defeat, victory and loss and loving, were no more than the moonlight falling across a sleeping face? And he himself would go unafraid and stand among the dark rushes and await the boatman, Charon, and stretch out his arms as so many before him had stretched out their arms with intense longing for the further shore. He whispered, lifting his arms slightly unknown to himself: '... *tendebantque manus ripae ulterioris amore.*' Of a sudden he became conscious of what he was doing. He jerked his mind back from the cold underworld and felt the evening sun warming his flesh with the ancient, temperate kindness. What had he been saying? What call had he, a man of the Faith, to be trafficking with the hell of pagans? Would he not die in peace, with the oil of the priest on his senses, his soul prepared? Aloud he said: 'Pagan or Christian, it's all the same. *Tendebantque manus ripae ulterioris amore.* Charon or Saint Peter!'

'Yes, that's it,' came a voice. 'That's right. You haven't forgotten it.'

'Eh! what's that? Did someone speak?'

'I say you haven't forgotten it.'

'Oh! Oh! yes, to be sure.' He turned his head sideways. 'You're the scholar, aren't you? No, son, I don't forget.' He paused diffidently. 'Did I say it right, word for word?'

'You said it although the sun was sending you to sleep.'

'Did I now? The sun, aye, the sun. It is the sun, isn't it?'

III

On a spring day, greyer and softer than the breast-plumage of a pigeon, they brought him his great-grandchild, a son, to the room where he now lay since the smoke in the kitchen troubled his lungs. Máire, the daughter, lifted him up against the pillows. He yawned mournfully and feebly scratched his chest. He took no notice of the people packed in the little space around the bed.

'Father, listen,' said the daughter patiently. 'Father, do you hear me? They're all here: Seumas and Seán and Brighed, and Sighle and her man with the new child. Father, don't you know

140

who he is? Your great-grandchild, father!'

He had his hands folded together, and he rubbed one thumb against the other unconcernedly. His chin was down, his mouth gaping to wheeze out the quick breaths.

Máire rubbed his forehead. 'Ah! father, do listen to me now. Don't you know who's here?'

'Who? Who? The priest, is it? Tell him I have no more sins for him. What does he think an old man can do?'

'It's Sighle and her new child.'

Seumas leaned down and placing his mouth near a waxen ear, said testily, 'It's your great-grandchild.'

The infant, frightened, was squawling, its puckered red face peeping out from the shawl.

'Put the child on his lap,' said Brighid.

Sighle held the child on the old man's lap. His hands came around and held the tiny body gently.

'What's this?' said he. 'What's this at all?'

'Your great-grandson,' they all said.

'I'm not deaf. I hear you. I hear you. He'll be a great man. A great man...'

The infant cried and dribbled. The old man did not move or speak, and his hands became still. They watched him silently and then Máire lifted his head. He was asleep.

IV

Only once more was he blessed with a spell of lucid days that, out of his ebbing lifetime, returned to him like a recoiling wave; and once more he sat, now wrapped in a blanket, in his elbow chair before the fire that would not have been burning so brightly but for his sake. The evening was hot on the house; the ditches were dry dust: but he could not be kept warm and he complained of the cold that made his hands and feet heavy and dead.

The household were at supper then, and they turned his chair till he faced them at the table.

'What,' he asked, 'were you doing with me down the room the other day?'

'It was your great-grandson we had,' Máire replied. 'You had him on your lap.'

'Had I?' he asked eagerly. 'I wasn't sure. I thought I heard in a dream the cry of a child. And his name?'

'Michael.'

'Hah! They didn't ask me for advice or for a name.'

'And how would you have named him?'

He moved his head from side to side and smiled weakly. 'Michael will do,' said he; and then, tapping on the wood of the chair: 'He'll see, I say, he'll see a different world. But it'll be full of our bones.'

'You should be a proud man,' Seumas remarked.

'A proud man!' he repeated, and bowed his chin into the folds of the blanket.

Over at the table they murmured, as they ate, about what neighbours had said or done and about the drought and, in a little while, about the fighting that seemed far off in the past like an old tale. To the same murmur, as level as the faint monotone of the insects hovering over the warm fields, they held their voices; for they thought that the man in the chair was sinking into a sleep. But then he spoke and the directness of his speech made them turn to listen and to watch.

'You said I should be a proud man,' said he. 'God knows I've been given many blessings, long years, children, and children's children, and a roof, and time to be prepared for death. Those are blessings indeed.' His speech failed to a muttering for a minute or two and then a fit of coughing almost overcame him altogether. Máire stood to go to his help; but hearing her step he waved her away with a long, thin, knuckled arm. 'But don't envy me,' he said clearly. 'I'm only sorry I have nothing to leave, for wealth never weighed me down. Maybe I'll leave a bad name, a name for wild fools and a warning. A fool I was in truth on many a day of my life, searching after things you'll not find in this world as I see now.' He twisted his mouth into a smile and shrugged his shoulders in the blanket. 'But it was pleasant to be a fool and I saw the best and the worst and...' They heard nothing but whispering and the voiceless sighing of his breath and when he spoke aloud again he said: 'But my feet are very cold, daughter. Very cold.'

V

Weakness crept over his flesh and enveloped him again and the body would respond no more. He took in a breath to call out, but thirst, festering in his throat, choked him. In no time, he thought, he found a cold spoon against his lips which he opened. His daughter was speaking. He drank.

'Water?' he asked.

'Yes! What else?'

'It's good. It has a good taste.'

He could not raise his arms and so she set him up against the pillow, feeling, as she did so, how light his body was, how it vibrated hollowly to the coughing, how close knit were the sinews and bones. She folded his arms on his chest and covered him up to the beard. He smiled and his slowly heavily opened eyes startled her for an instant. She fancied that he had seen. Then, leaving him, she closed the door and said to herself a prayer that he would get a good night's sleep.

He heard the click of the door-catch and he lay quiet. A hissing like the sea in a shell bothered his hearing, and to banish it, he rocked his head slightly on the pillow. He would have to hear them now and to talk with them. They were all coming down into the room. If only one of them would give him a spoon of water, icy clear sparkling water like the streams that streaked the dark mountains with silver in the spring. The light became so fluffy with a dark grey haze that even the sound of footfalls was less than the movement of a hand through the air. More faces than he had time to recognise passed round him, passing away into the outer encircling gloom, returning solemnly and with a kindness of feature that went to his heart and brought tears to his eyes. This, he thought, is no hosting for Charon, no mobbing of souls in a frenzy of fear and longing but the ample, compassionate companionship of the dead, coming for one of their own, and he began to pray, gathering up his powers to a pin-point as a man musters up his strength and bunches his muscles to crash from the ring of his enemies. He relaxed for another effort. Like gulls poising on upper currents of the wind, words floated lightly: *per istam sanctam unctionem*... and suddenly, his senses were clear. He heard, distinctly. The room was empty and for one instant he felt the breeze from the window passing coolly across his face, his eyes and his mouth.

AN CEANGAL

It was late when Donnacha, the son, arrived. He went below to the room, said his prayers with head down, stood for a minute staring stolidly at the gaunt, sunken face and returned to the kitchen. A place was made for him on a form beside the fire among the older men where, in the silence and the clouding pungent tobacco smoke, he ate bread and meat and drank the ale provided for the wake. All the night, people walked back and forth on tip-toe between the kitchen door and the lower room where the dead lay, the mouth shut firm, the eyelids down, the body small and narrow beneath the white coverlet. On the morrow they would bring him to Newtown for burial as he had wished and men would take turns to carry the coffin that stood, unlidded and gaping, on its end at the foot of the bed.

'Your father,' said a greybeard to the son, 'your father was a man who won't be forgotten for many a long day.' He looked around for approval, shaking his head emphatically and accepting the assenting nods with a repeated, 'Faith, it's true, it's true.' Around by the walls men took the pipes from their mouths and spoke, one after the other, gently and with unwinking remembering eyes. They were weaving with words a habit for the dead.

'A poet he was. A good poet.'

'Only yesterday I heard his song about the hills of Ireland, and a young girl was singing it in Newtown.'

'He made it before most of us were born.'

'It will meet him at the grave.'

'There was never any harm in him at all.'

'No; never. Never a bit.'

'And a fine schoolmaster.'

'There aren't many of his kind left in the land.'

'Or in any other land, I'll swear.'

'Oh! the stories that could be told, but only himself could tell them.'

'I recall one time,' began the greybeard again, 'when himself and myself and three others were down in the tavern. Now, he'd not be angry,' added the teller, glancing across at the candlelit door, and pointing with the stem of his pipe, 'he'd not be angry with me, I know, for telling this story. There are more stories about him than will ever be told.' They moved closer to the fire and leaned forward and stared. 'Well, we were all in the tavern, with not even a red penny between us, when a foreign traveller rode up and...'

The candles smoked and wavered beside the bed and the only life on the still, white face was the flickering dance of the shadows.

Crioch.